Courteous, courageous and commanding—
these heroes lay it all on the line for the
people they love in more than fifty stories about
loyalty, bravery and romance.
Don't miss a single one!

New York Times and
USA TODAY Bestselling Author

KATHLEEN EAGLE

BAD MOON RISING

Published by Silhouette Books
America's Publisher of Contemporary Romance

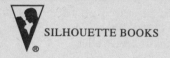

SILHOUETTE BOOKS

Recycling programs for this product may not exist in your area.

ISBN-13: 978-0-373-36256-1

BAD MOON RISING

Copyright © 1991 by Kathleen Eagle

This edition published by arrangement with Harlequin Books S.A.

For questions and comments about the quality of this book please contact us at Customer_eCare@Harlequin.ca.

® and TM are trademarks of Harlequin Books S.A., used under license. Trademarks indicated with ® are registered in the United States Patent and Trademark Office, the Canadian Trade Marks Office and in other countries.

Visit Silhouette Books at www.eHarlequin.com

Printed in U.S.A.

KATHLEEN EAGLE

published her first book, a Romance Writers of America Golden Heart Award winner, with Silhouette Books in 1984. Since then she has published more than forty books, including historical and contemporary, series and single title, earning her nearly every award in the industry. Her books have consistently appeared on regional and national bestseller lists, including the *USA TODAY* list and the *New York Times* extended bestseller list.

Kathleen lives in Minnesota with her husband, who is Lakota Sioux. They have three grown children and three lively grandchildren.

For Bob and Connie Charette.
Thanks for sharing an experience
that gave me some of the background for this story.

Thanks to friends and relatives
who have blessed me with some insight into
the contemporary Lakota Sioux experience.

Special thanks to Chris Dill, Mark Halvorson
and Todd Strand of the Historical Society of
North Dakota, for their continued willingness
to make the state's historic treasures accessible.

Chapter 1

The brown horse grunted with the strain of trying to pop George Tracker off his back, but George was a cowboy. Added years and pounds hadn't diminished Gorgeous George's looks, nor his bronc-busting style. At least, not in his sister's eyes.

Frances Tracker balanced herself on the top rail of their father's corral and cheered him on—"Ride 'em, Gorgeous!"—just like old times. The battered straw hat took a tumble, but George hung in there. His thick mop of black hair glistened in the slanted rays of the evening sun, and his blue nylon windbreaker billowed like a parachute with each jump. The snaky colt that had flopped brothers Beaver and Tom Tom last week had met its match now that the older boys were home. Frankie whooped and churned a fist in the air to let her brother know that he was still the same old Gorgeous George.

Other onlookers would notice the way George's belly-roll bounced, and once he was on the ground, they would probably tease him. Frances wouldn't. She was already sorting out the superlatives with which to praise him. Piggybacked to those would be an offer to trim his hair for him before he went out tonight.

"Eeee-yo! Stick with him, Gorgeous!"

Their oldest brother, Luke, added his whistle to Frankie's cheers. Grimacing, Luke's wife clapped a hand over the ear her husband's voice had assailed. From the far side of the corral, Frankie had no trouble reading the apology on Luke's lips, and his sheepish grin made her giggle. No more Sergeant Stoneface. He was still a soldier, but Sergeant Luke Tracker's barracks days were over. Hope was the right woman for him, even if she was a *wasicu,* a white woman. Hope had come to their South Dakota reservation from the East Coast to teach third grade—one grade up from the class Frankie handled—and she was great with the children.

Actually, right now she was great with *child,* and Luke had been stuck to her side like peanut butter ever since they'd been home on leave. Well, she wasn't *that* great, Frankie amended as she watched George wave his free hand above his head, riding high. But Hope was definitely showing. It was a little early for the gingham maternity top, but you could tell she would really need it soon. And Frankie—even though she had no desire whatever to be saddled with a husband and a bunch of kids—wondered what her sister-in-law's condition really felt like. Most women her age, the ones she knew, had already found out for themselves several times over. Frankie figured it was natural to wonder about it. Just wondering had never gotten anybody pregnant.

They both looked happy, and Frankie took a piece of the credit for that. Fixing him up with a wife had been one way to get Luke to come home on leave once in a while. A year ago Christmas had been the first time in seven years. Frankie had brought Hope home for the holidays, and that was that.

They had planned a Christmas wedding, but what with both of them burning up the highways and airways between South Dakota and Fort Leonard Wood, Missouri, every chance they got, they'd tied the knot on Thanksgiving. Hope had finished out her second year of teaching in Wakpala, the little reservation town not far from the Tracker ranch. As soon as school was out, almost three months ago now, Luke had come home to take his new bride back to his post. But she was further along than three months, so Frankie figured one of those rendezvous in Kansas City in the spring must have been pretty okay. This time, after fourteen years in the army, Luke was transferring overseas with a family.

As for Gorgeous George, well, he'd always been a worry. He would shack up with one woman, quit her, then find another. And he was always partying like there was no tomorrow. Lately, though, things had changed. He'd moved back home. He said it was only temporary, just until he got his new business on its feet. He didn't talk about the business much, because he knew people wouldn't take him seriously, but he'd told Frankie about it. Some kind of construction, and he even had a partner. He had a new girlfriend, too, but he was talking even less about that. Still, he'd told Frankie. He always told Frankie.

The bronc's high kicking wound down to a choppy

crow-hop. George's free hand came down slowly as he tapped the horse's flanks with his boot heels, checking to see if he had any more gas.

"All done now?" George asked the horse. His pudgy, grinning face was bathed in sweat, and that windbreaker over his T-shirt didn't help matters on such a muggy evening. But George was a cowboy, and good cowboys wore long sleeves when they rode broncs.

"Looks like you took all the buck out of him, Gorgeous," Frankie judged as she clambered down from her perch. She smacked Tom Tom's butt as she sashayed past the two younger boys, who sat side by side on the rail, chattering like a pair of scrawny magpies. "See there?" Frankie demanded. "You boys see how it's done? You've gotta stick him till he gives up."

"Plus—" Dragging his sleeve across his face, George took a moment to wheeze a little. Once he'd caught his breath, he made his point buoyantly as he pulled his rigging off the colt's back. "You've gotta be smarter than the horse you're trying to break."

"Yeah, well…"

"Well, what?" Frankie shaded her eyes with one hand and planted the other on her hip as she squinted up at the two. Her long black braid dangled down her back.

Beaver was almost a man, but in the presence of his three older siblings, he still felt like a kid. He had to come up with some kind of a wise comeback. "You'd stop bucking, too, if you had something as big as him on your back."

"Aw, Beaver, you wound me." George thumped his chest, then grinned for his audience as he hoisted the rigging over his shoulder and sauntered across the dusty arena. "'Course, I've heard all about how many times that horse flopped you boys, so I guess it still takes an old wrangler like me to show you how to top one off."

He dropped the rigging next to the split-rail fence and peered over the top, posturing like a teapot. "Don't think he'll give you any trouble if you wanna try him out, Luke."

"Think I'll pass. You're the bronc rider, Gorgeous." Everyone waited. Like Frankie, they all knew there would be more. Luke grinned. "How about a little one-on-one?"

"Hey, yeah," Tom Tom chimed in. "Let's get a game up."

"I better be gettin'." George climbed the fence and heaved himself over the top, then dropped to the ground on the outside. He peeled off the nylon shell, taking care to puff out his chest in the process. "I'm the bronc rider. Luke's the buckets expert. He'll get up a game with you guys."

Beaver jumped down to retrieve the rigging, which he'd gotten out after he'd challenged George to buck the colt out. He knew he was expected to put the equipment away.

But Tom Tom wasn't giving up. "C'mon, Gorgeous. With Luke, we got enough for two teams if we let the girls play."

Frankie laughed. "Who says we wanna play?"

"They're not counting you," Luke told his wife.

Hope patted her rounded tummy and exchanged a bright-eyed smile with her husband. "Why not? They can even count me twice."

"See there?" George punched Luke's shoulder. "Hope and Little Sarge can fill in for me. I gotta shower up and get going." He looked up at Tom Tom, who was still straddling the fence. "You wanna turn that horse out, or keep him in and finish the job?"

No answer was required. The gauntlet was down, and the horse would be green-broke inside a week.

"What's your hurry?" Luke asked. "Hot date?" George returned a guarded look, a message between brothers. Luke cocked an eyebrow. "Really?"

"She ain't hot, Sarge. She's real cool and sweet."

"His manners must be improving, then," Luke said in a theatrical aside to his wife. "He never used to mind keeping them waiting."

"Not this lady." George wasn't joking anymore. He glanced at Frankie, who knew and understood. "I'm in love, brother. Just like you."

"No kidding? Anybody I know?"

"Uh, sort of. Maybe."

He was easing away now. Frankie knew that telling Luke would be hard for him. Years had passed, but that was still just the way it was. Later, after Frankie had explained, it would be easier for George to broach the subject with his brother. Frankie thought of her part as a kind of warm-up.

"I'm gonna jump in the shower real quick." George gave his sister the nod and the usual go-ahead. "You tell him."

Frankie laughed as George trotted off toward the mostly white, two-story house. She'd always been the message carrier, peacemaker and apologist for her two older brothers. She didn't mind. She understood them better than they understood themselves. Luke and George, like day and night, one always crowding in on the other. She played both dawn and dusk.

"You remember Lannie Latimer?"

Luke chortled. "Lannie Latimer!"

"Don't." Frankie raised a warning hand.

Luke glanced furtively toward the house, lowered his voice and tried again. "Lannie Latimer? She's kind of, uh…old, isn't she?"

"That's not what came to your head first. What you're thinking is, she's not exactly *gorgeous.*"

"Not exactly cool, either."

Frankie exchanged glances with Hope, letting her know, just between women, that a Plain Jane was under attack by an insensitive male. Hope folded her arms, and Luke was cornered. The couple's cause, if it needed defending, was a natural for her, too. He backed down, shaking his head. "I don't even remember what she looked like, to tell you the truth. She was Trey's older sister. That's all I remember."

Trey Latimer. Frankie dismissed the connection with a grimace. She could accept George's new lady friend just fine if she forgot that the woman was Trey Latimer's sister. She wasn't sure why, after all this time. She'd had a schoolgirl crush on her big brother's best friend. No big deal.

"I just know she was *older,*" Luke restated.

"Not by that much."

"Jeez, Trey Latimer. I haven't seen Trey since we graduated from high school," Luke said. "We used to have some good times. But then we went our separate ways. Both of us dying to blow this pop stand. See what the real world was like."

"Well, he's back, from what I hear." She hadn't seen him, but then, she wasn't looking for him, either. The Latimers had a fancy house overlooking the Missouri River from the west side. That put them on the reservation, even though they were just a stone's throw from Mobridge, which was a white town. *Their* town, east of the river. The river was the demarcation between two worlds, and Frankie thought the west side was an interesting spot for old man Latimer to have built his showplace, considering. "I guess the Latimers aren't real pleased about this romance budding between their Lannie and our George."

"I remember feeling the same way about *their* Trey and *our* Frankie," Luke recalled.

Her face felt warm. "That was different."

"Maybe. I knew Trey pretty well then." Luke slipped one arm around his sister's shoulders, the other around his wife's. "And I know George. Next time I come home, he'll be telling me about his *new* old lady."

"Didn't you notice? He didn't call her his *old* lady. He just said *lady*."

They were shuffling along now, the three of them, but not toward the house. The sultriness, unusual for the high plains except on a rare summer night, felt even worse inside the house. It was the shady squaw cooler— the Indian gazebo, made from poles and leafy tree branches—that beckoned.

"You don't know him as well as you think you do, Luke. He gave her flowers last week."

That drew an incredulous look.

"Hey, it happens." Frankie smiled and unearthed one of her favorite digs. "How's Hope's Christmas kitten?"

"You mean Noelle?" Hope said. She broke off a willow twig as they ducked beneath the dry thatch. The leaves rattled, then went still again. Hope teased Luke's chin with the twig, and the look in his eyes reminded Frankie of the time Luke's Christmas offering had exposed his soft heart. "Sweet as can be," Hope said wistfully.

Luke's smile was warm, even as he complained, "We had to hire a damn sitter for a cat."

Hope turned to Frankie. "After the wedding you get fewer flowers and kittens, more kitchen appliances."

"Hey, what about that lacy, black—"

"And nightgowns," Hope admitted. "They do like to pick out your nightgowns."

Frankie tried to imagine Luke in a women's lingerie department sorting through filmy nighties. She couldn't. If she hadn't seen it with her own eyes, she wouldn't have believed he would give a woman a kitten for Christmas, either. Not Luke. That was a bigger surprise than George's flowers. She wondered what it was about white women that inspired this kind of sentimentality. Nobody had ever given Frankie any flowers. Not that she wanted any. They would just die pretty quick anyway. But she kind of wondered what it would be like to have someone—a man—give them to her.

Hope could keep the cat, though.

George emerged from the house a changed man. The cowboy was on his way to the city, walking like a man who had eggs in his boots. Frankie managed to maintain a straight face, but the new look was very un-Gorgeous. George wore brand-new jeans and a crisp white Western shirt that looked as though it might still have a piece of cardboard tucked under the collar. If his date lacked "cool," George would be a fine match. Frankie remembered the haircut she'd intended to offer, but decided not to say anything that might take the gleam out of her brother's eyes. He was doing so damn good lately, and she was proud of him.

"Would you take a look at Slick, here." Luke made the traditional production of taking a whiff of George's after-shave as soon as he ventured close enough. "Jeez, give the woman a fighting chance."

"Don't pay any attention to him, George," Hope said. She was sitting in an aluminum lawn chair. A strip of green webbing, loose from the seat, dragged in the prairie grass stubble beneath her. "That's a great shirt."

"Thanks. We're just going to the show, maybe having some supper."

"Pretty low-key for you, Gorgeous." Luke propped his booted foot on the seat of a folding chair. He looked more comfortable in his short-sleeved shirt than George did in his stiff new long-sleeved one. Frankie wished George would roll his sleeves and loosen up a little. But not too much—not the way he used to.

"I like it that way. So does Lannie." George grinned. "I sort of have to steer clear of her dad, 'cause we don't want a big fuss. I've been a hell-raiser for a long time. Everybody knows that. But that's all changing." He paused, then confided, "I haven't had a drink in three months, Luke."

The brothers looked at each other for a moment. It was Luke's face that Frankie watched, looking for a change of expression that was slow in coming. She chafed. Didn't he believe George? She wanted to back her brother up, but she waited.

Wordlessly, Luke offered George his hand, and George took it, smiling.

"I got to know Lannie at the bank," George said. "She works there and—" he chuckled self-consciously "—I got my own account now. You believe that?"

"Sure I do," Luke said.

"I'll go you a little one-on-one tomorrow, okay?" Luke nodded, and George, with a pointed glance at Hope, confided, "I want what you've got."

He always had, and that was Frankie's one concern.

Ever since she could remember, George had always
tried to follow Luke. The cowboy had worn the basketball shoes his older brother had outgrown. Later he'd
tried the combat boots on for size. They hadn't fit. And
whenever George failed, he failed big. It was his way
of making his mark.

Now he was all dressed up for courting the shy bank
teller with the pale, thin hands. He was wearing his own
cowboy boots, but...holy moly, they were *polished.*

"Will you look at that!" George said as he stepped
away from the squaw cooler. The other three turned
obediently. They'd been facing the house, backs to the
expansive prairie. A big orange moon rose above the
buttes, floating like a champagne bubble. "That is one
bad moonrise. Bet you anything we get some heat lightning tonight. Thunderstorm, maybe."

There were no clouds, but the air was thick and
heavy, too lazy to move. The prairie would not tolerate
the stillness long.

"Sure sign of trouble," Luke said.

"Not for me," George said. He headed for his old blue
pickup with a parting promise. "My troublemaking days
are over. You guys take it easy."

Fifteen miles away, Trey Latimer also took notice of
the big orange moon on the rise above the river and
thought about the traditional predictions. He'd grown up
with them. In the Dakotas, people paid a lot of attention
to the sky, because there was so damn much of it. But
the eerie August moonrise hardly seemed foreboding to
Trey, since his troubles were already pounding against
the walls of his skull.

Maybe the full moon had something to do with the

timing of the riptide that was dragging his brain down
for the count as he headed for the red pickup he'd parked
in his father's driveway. But he knew the moon wasn't
the cause. He owed his particular brand of lunacy to a
metal plate planted beneath the scar that started above
his right eyebrow and disappeared into his dark blond
hair. That and the old man's persistent inability to see
past the end of his own beak. A hot, still night like this
one was a breeder of storms, like the one he'd just
walked out on. But that kind of trouble was nothing new.

"Trey! Wait up."

The screen door slapped shut behind his younger
brother. Trey hesitated, his hand poised to open the pickup
door as he watched Race descend the porch steps effort-
lessly, like a cat. Race's stubbornness was almost a match
for the old man's. Nobody could tell him anything. Cross
him, and he had a temper that wouldn't quit. Race Latimer
should have been his father's chosen heir. But he wasn't.
He'd been born too late, born of the wrong mother.

"Trey, listen." Trey didn't want to hear it, but this was
Race, after all, and not their father. Trey was the prodigal
son returned but not quite humbled, at least in Phillip
Latimer's eyes. But Trey still held out hope for family
ties of some kind, with somebody. His sister Lannie.
Maybe Race. He hoped he could be friends with Race.

Race offered a cigarette, but Trey shook it off. The
smoke would only add grist to the mill grinding away
inside his head. Race lit up, then started into his case.

"The old man's right. Lannie's making a fool of
herself in her old age, and we've gotta put a stop to it."

Trey couldn't help laughing. In ten years Race would
remember the remark and laugh, too. "She's all of thirty-
six, which isn't exactly 'old age.'"

"Hell, you know what I mean. She's what you might call…"

"An old maid?" Trey shook his head, chuckling humorlessly. Poor Lannie. She should have moved out to Denver when he'd asked her to, about the time his daughter was born, which would have been almost seven years ago. "What rock have you and Dad been hiding under? There's no shame in being single. Women don't have to get married these days if they don't want to."

"Yeah, well, Lannie *wants* to. She must be desperate." Race's black eyes glittered. "George Tracker's a joke, Trey. You know, Luke's pretty…" At the mention of his old friend's name, Trey shot a warning glance. Race shifted his boot heels on the pavement. "Luke's different. George is…hell, have you ever seen that guy tie one on? You want your sister tied up with some lowlife who goes around—"

"That's her business."

"The hell it is. He better not let me catch him with her." Race dropped his cigarette and crushed it beneath his boot heel as he dug his keys out of the pocket of his tight-fitting jeans.

"Where are you going?"

"I'm meeting some friends."

Trey closed his eyes and rubbed his temples with one hand, thumb on one side, fingertips on the other. The pain wrecked his train of thought. "Leave Lannie alone, Race. It's like I just told—" he waved his hand toward the house "—*him*. She's had little enough happiness in her life."

"Oh, come on. You really think George Tracker is anybody's idea of Prince Charming?"

"Leave it alone, Race. Let her decide for herself."

They gave each other a moment's worth of stony

stares before Race raised both hands in surrender and smiled. "Hey. Let's go get us a beer. I'm buying."

"Can't." Damn his crazy head, he didn't want to turn Race down. It was a peace offering, and Trey wanted peace more than anything these days. He clapped a hand on his brother's shoulder and returned the smile as best he could. "Gotta run my mares in. This kind of weather… Look at that damn moon. Feels like something's coming."

"You were a cop too long. You're always expecting something." Race started down the driveway. The glitter in his eyes now was pure mischief. "If it starts lightning, get that tin head of yours inside, okay?"

"You—" That was the look that reminded Trey of Luke and George Tracker. Even Frankie, their sister. The knockout smile that started in his brother's eyes. "Stay out of trouble."

"Right."

Chapter 2

A dewy spider web in the corner of the overhang above the back door glinted with a touch of morning sunlight. Frankie wondered how it had survived the storm. Broken cottonwood branches were strewn around the yard, attesting to the power of the wind. Cottonwoods were easily broken, easily regenerated, and the wind had blown itself out. A night full of thunder made you think the roof might fall in, but the sturdy old house and the spider's web were both standing, making nighttime fears seem silly by daylight. The heaviness had been lifted from the air. The day would be hot, but dry.

It must have been three in the morning when she'd heard the thunder bomb, followed quickly by her ten-year-old sister Sweetie's feet scrabbling across the floor. Frankie had scooted to the edge of the twin bed and let Sweetie crawl over her and claim her favorite spot next to the wall. Then she'd slid into a strangely fragmented and oppressive dream. Morning had been a welcome relief.

Now she tuned in to the familiar *thud-thud-thud-whap-thunk* that had always been a sign of life around the Tracker place. Somebody was shooting baskets out back. There were square bales out in the hay field, too wet to haul this morning. In the evening Daddy would load up a crew of kids to go out and turn them all over to dry on the bottom. But for now there was a lone early-bird getting in some practice shots at the hoop with the raggedy net and the makeshift backboard, bolted to an old telephone pole in the big, bare yard.

Frankie stepped outside quietly, since most of the household was still asleep. They'd played rummy last night until after midnight. Tom Tom was the diehard. Last to bed, first one up. He wasn't going to let any of his brothers get by him without at least shooting a few free throws in a game of "Horse." He would soon be as good as Luke, maybe better, and he was dying for Luke to tell him so.

With everyone home the house was crowded, just like old times. Good times. Even the old outhouse was getting some use again when the line for the bathroom got too long. But soon Luke and Hope would be on their way to Germany. Frankie would go back to her little apartment in Wakpala and get ready for school to start. And George...who could tell about Gorgeous George? Maybe he'd actually settle down.

Frankie had errands to run. The family of thirteen had been going through coffee and flour like tomorrow wasn't coming. The quick, hard downpour had left some puddles, but the water had drained away from the hard-packed high ground in the clay yard where Tom Tom was lining up a corner shot. Frankie paused on her way to the blue hatchback, which was parked in the shade of her father's old black pickup. Tom Tom made the swish, then shot her a grin.

"Can't you get anybody to play this morning?" she asked.

"Luke and Beaver aren't up yet, and I don't know where George is."

"Didn't come home last night?"

"Nope." Tom Tom dribbled twice and made a turn-around shot.

So much for Gentleman George. "Go easy on Luke. They're leaving tomorrow, and he'll be trying to spread himself pretty thin today, since we won't be seeing him for a while."

"You going to town?" She was already on her way. "Bring me back a can of snuff."

"In your dreams," she tossed back.

"Hey, I've got money."

"Buy it yourself, then."

"Give it up, Frankie. School don't start again for four weeks."

He was dribbling and she was driving away, watching him model a dark scowl for the benefit of her mirror view. He could have done something worse. She chuckled at the holes in the knees of his faded blue jeans. They were in style now, which was kind of nice. They were as much an equalizer as the gray-and-white uniform she'd had to wear the year she'd been per-suaded to go away to a mission school. One year had been all she could take. She'd asked her father not to send her back, promised she would get straight A's and stop fighting if he would let her come back home and

attend Wakpala's little public school. She knew it wasn't
easy to keep everybody at home fed and clothed, and
everybody said she'd get a better education if she went
away to boarding school. But homesickness hurt really
bad sometimes. So they'd made the bargain. She had
almost kept it, too, except for a few B's and C's.

Frankie took it easy as she approached the big bend
in the three-quarter-mile dirt road that connected the
house with the highway. There was one big hole ahead,
and her little car would probably bottom out if she hit
it wrong. As she skirted the brown puddle, she caught
a glimpse of something white lying near the mailbox.
It looked like a shirt. And a boot—*two* boots. Frankie
pulled over. There was somebody lying there, about
twenty feet from the blacktop.

She left the car running, but she couldn't make her
own feet move very fast. Sunflowers and curling switch-
grass shielded the body from view, but she had a bad
feeling. It was the kind of feeling she always had trouble
shaking after she'd had one of her dreams. She knew she
had dreamed this face, cracked like a mirror and not
quite recognizable. Now it was daylight, and the dream
was concluded. This was George.

Tears came quickly, even before she turned him over.
His new shirt was torn at the shoulder. He had fallen off
the wagon, facedown into the roadside right-of-way.
He reeked of alcohol. "You were doing so good," she
whispered to him. "Now you'll have to start all—"

Oh, God.

His face had been pulverized! There was blood
everywhere, coming from his nose and his mouth.

"What happened?" she said, touching, drawing back,
looking for a place to touch. "What hap—"

No more tears now. She had to find a pulse some-where. She found his wrist. "Oh, God, please let me find it. Please. I know he's alive. See? He feels warm."

Nothing.

"Please, please, where is it?"

Nothing.

Then something. A flutter, yes, a little sign.

"Somebody! George is hurt! Somebody!"

She didn't want to leave him alone, but nobody could hear her, and she couldn't lift him.

Help. Help. She stumbled through the tall grass, laid into the horn, then darted back and felt for that thready pulse again. It would be just like him to try to slip away while she wasn't looking. It was there, still there.

"Somebody help! George is hurt!"

Were they coming? She clambered into the car, threw it into Reverse and struggled with the door, the steering wheel, the accelerator and the horn, all at once. She forgot about puddles and potholes, ignored the bend in the road. The rear tires hit the ditch with a thud. She switched into first gear and burned rubber. Her horn sounded like the high-pitched shriek of a desperate child.

"Help me, please." *Somebody. Somebody.*

Tom Tom appeared at the side of the house, then Luke's white T-shirt brightened the top of the screen door.

"It's George! He's hurt!"

Even though they couldn't hear her, they understood that there was trouble. The brothers converged on their father's pickup. As Luke slowed it down, Frankie leaped from her car onto the running board, shouting orders.

It was the torn shirt that stuck in Frankie's mind as she waited on the bench across from the nurses' station at the Mobridge Hospital. A stupid little thing, considering how many shirts George had torn over the years and how many she'd conspired to mend in the hope that Mama wouldn't notice. But she sat there staring at the white walls and thought about that white shirt. She wished now that she'd offered to iron it for him, because the woman—if he'd actually met up with the woman—must have noticed that the shirt had just been taken from the package and maybe thought he didn't know any better. It was so white, that shirt. Brand-new.

The police were talking to Luke now, thank God. Frankie had told them everything three times, at least. She didn't know where George had been. She didn't know where his pickup was. She *did* know that somebody had beaten him up and dumped him near their mailbox. Did they think he'd gotten there on his own?

She also knew that he was supposed to have been with Lannie Latimer. Yes, *Latimer.*

"Um, excuse me. Frances?"

Speak of the devil. Not that she had anything *against* Lannie Latimer—and it was nice to hear her own given name for a change—but Lannie sure didn't seem like Gorgeous's type. Too soft-looking, for one thing, the way she was standing there with that little purse strap hitched over her wrist, hands clasped. Frankie acknowledged her by raising her head.

"Where…where's George?"

Something inside Frankie wanted to keep George's battered face and tattered clothes from this timid woman. But she answered, "They took him from the emergency room into X-ray."

"What happened?"

"We don't know. He won't—" She was angry with

him, too, and she knew it made no sense. She'd sat in the bed of the pickup, hunching over him, calling to him, but he'd just lain there like a big lump. Wouldn't open his eyes, wouldn't answer.

Frankie took a cleansing breath. "He's unconscious. We don't know. Wasn't he with you last night?"

"Yes. Until about midnight. Will they let me see him?"

"My dad's..." With a nod Frankie indicated the corridor down which the nurses had directed her father. Then she noticed Trey Latimer standing near the nurses' station, straw cowboy hat in hand, listening.

She stopped and stared, and he stared back.

Trey Latimer.

He hadn't changed much. He still looked as though he'd fit right in with the Beach Boys. She wondered why he hadn't moved to California after high school instead of Colorado. Probably because he was no bebopping surfer, for all his golden-haired good looks. No matter what kind of a job he'd had, he was the same kind of big-headed, redneck cowboy who was sure to get away with beating up her brother.

Trey started to give her that tentative you-remember-me smile. She came to her senses and looked away.

"Maybe I could talk with your father," Lannie suggested in a voice not much stronger than a small breeze. "They won't tell me much, because I'm not family."

"They won't tell us much, either."

"Maybe after they finish with the X-rays," Lannie suggested hopefully. "Do you think they'll let us see him then?"

Us? "My father's waiting by the door. They said they'd tell him if George comes to, so he's waiting by the X-ray room."

"Did George tell you…about us?"

Another *us*. Frankie remembered the look on George's face when he'd talked about his "lady." She had to be fair to the woman now, for George's sake. Accept her for face value, she told herself. This Lannie of the long, narrow face, bulging blue eyes and thin yellow hair was nobody's fair maiden, but her distress was evident in the way she kept pulling on her hand, as though she were milking a cow.

Then came the unbidden thought. How had this skinny thing ever gotten to be Trey Latimer's sister?

Frankie resisted the temptation to glance past his sister, this time to invite from him the well-remembered flirtatious smile. Instead she took pity on Lannie by giving her the news she wanted. "He's been telling me lately that he's really in love." Lannie's face lit up too easily. "Of course, George has always been kind of—" Frankie couldn't do it. This one was too vulnerable. "He's kind of romantic, isn't he? Deep down."

Lannie offered a dewy-eyed smile. "He's so sweet. How could anyone hurt him like that? He's such a sweet, gentle man."

"Come on," Frankie offered, taking Lannie by the arm. "Let's go talk to Daddy."

When Frankie returned, having left Lannie to share George Senior's quiet vigil near the door to the X-ray lab, she found Trey Latimer still posted near the nurses' station. He'd put his straw cowboy hat back on, and she was surprised he hadn't left. He said something to the pretty blond nurse who was manning the station, and she smiled, which explained everything.

But then he turned from the desk and crossed the tiled floor in her direction.

"It's good to see you again, Frankie. Except, not like this."

How, then? she wondered. He'd usually treated her as the "kid sister," and she'd always been able to anticipate his first question. "Luke's in the staff room, talking to the police."

"I saw him." He shoved his hands into the pockets of his jeans. "Actually, they're finished in there now. He took your brother Tom over to the drive-in to get him something to eat. The kid was about ready to faint."

"Tom Tom," Frankie corrected. Trey rewarded her with a quizzical expression. "His name's not Tom. It's really Preston. We just call him Tom Tom."

"I guess I always assumed it really was Tom."

"No. Just one of those kid things." And proof that Trey Latimer wasn't in with the Trackers. Not anymore. "I heard you've moved back from Denver."

"I've been back for about six months now, but I haven't seen too many—well, I ran into your sisters in town one day. Dolly and, uh…"

He searched for a name, but she knew he wouldn't come up with it. "Crystal," she supplied. The girls had told her about their encounter with him, and Dolly had made a big deal about what a hunk he was. *Still* was. She should never have told Dolly anything. In those days, all senior boys had been "hunks." All six of them.

He smiled, as though recalling the name were actually important to him. "She must have been the baby when I left, but she said there were two more after her." Frankie had it in her head to ask him if he wanted to make something of it, but he cut her off. "That's great. You have quite a family, Frankie."

"Yes." She didn't want any part of what she was

feeling. Not now. Thinking back on the way he'd once made her adolescent heart flutter was an embarrassment even under the best of circumstances, and she didn't want to be interested in any damn thing this golden man had to say. But she prompted him anyway, with, "So you're back to stay?"

"I bought a little place out by Rattlesnake Butte, and I've been pretty busy trying to get set up." He glanced down the corridor. "I brought Lannie over."

Frankie nodded. "Bad news travels fast. Who called her?"

"I heard the police call," he explained. "I'm filling in temporarily as county sheriff until they elect someone in November. Bob Mackie moved away, you know."

"No, I didn't." Nor did she care. That whole county courthouse bunch seemed like a redundancy on the reservation. The tribe had its own Department of Law and Order, its own police force. But there were non-Indians on the reservation, and there was non-Indian land within its boundaries. She supposed they needed their sheriff.

"Found a job that paid better, which couldn't have been too hard." He smiled, and she noticed that he really had changed. He'd aged, just like everyone else. Maybe *matured* was a better word. It was in his eyes, mostly. Cares, weariness, experience. Some of that bright blue she remembered seemed to have faded. His eyes were gray now.

"Anyway, they had to appoint someone," he continued. "I agreed to it because they promised there wouldn't be much to it. The Indian police handle most of the business."

"Unless, by chance, a non-Indian should commit a crime."

"Well, sure," he said, lifting one shoulder as if such a thing should be self-evident. "But Corson County looks pretty peaceful to somebody coming from a city the size of Denver."

"Peaceful," she repeated, weighing the word. How often had Gorgeous been accused of disturbing the peace? She wondered whether *unconscious* might be considered peaceful, too, and she asked, "Will you be looking for the people who did this thing to my brother?"

His hesitancy didn't surprise her. "If they ask me to. So far I guess it's under the B.I.A.'s jurisdiction. I haven't talked to anybody yet, but from what I heard on the radio—"

"Red tape," she said, and they looked at each other for a moment. He knew what she was talking about, but she explained anyway. "It'll all get bogged down in red tape. Nobody will be able to do anything, because it'll be someone else's job." His eyes offered sympathy, but she wanted none of it. "Is that the way it is in Denver? Weren't you a cop out there for a while?"

"Yeah. I was a cop." It sounded like an admission of something, maybe failure or regret. Whatever it was had taken the amiable brightness out of his eyes. "There's red tape there, too."

She expected nothing from him, so she didn't know why the fact that he offered no help should make her feel any more desolate. But there was something in his eyes, in the tone of his voice, that said he shared her frustration in some way. Maybe he had no help to give. Maybe nobody did. Her chest felt tight. She wanted to be angry now, but instead she was scared.

"Listen, it'll be okay," he offered. "George will be able to tell us who did this."

"I don't know." She shook her head and glanced away from him. Her throat burned, but she wasn't going to get teary. Not Frankie. "He looks like he's asleep, you know? You want to yell at him to make him—"

His hand rose tentatively, just like the smile he'd attempted earlier, as if he half expected her to shrug him away. She should have. She didn't need pity. But her mind was filled with images of George, and when she looked up at Trey, she saw gray-eyed, world-weary understanding. She permitted herself to lean toward him, and his arms went around her.

He spoke softly. "I always thought of Luke as your big brother, but George is, too. Good ol' Gorgeous George. Luke's tail."

"But he wouldn't hurt a fly."

"That's a good one, Frankie. We'll have to tell him that one." His chuckle was a reminder of the way things were supposed to be. Tails were supposed to swat flies. "As soon as he comes to, he'll be joking around, too."

"I wasn't joking. I meant…" He knew what she meant, but he also remembered Gorgeous George, she realized, and the way he had of finding humor in the worst possible mess. Words had double meanings, and George could drive you crazy with them. But not now that he lay so quiet and still. "He looked awful," she whispered against the Western-cut flap of Trey's shirt pocket. "His face was all blood and dirt and—" She looked up. "He can't stay like that. He has to wake up."

"You only hear about the people who don't come out of something like this, but lots of people do. I did."

"You?"

He almost smiled as he touched the scar on his forehead. "I was out for four days."

"What happened?"

"I got shot. It was pretty freaky." While the reserves were down, he permitted her to look closely, and she allowed him to hold her shoulders in his hands and bolster her spirits. "You have to keep the faith, Frankie. I know damn well George's head is just as hard as mine."

It was Luke who shattered the moment with an innocent rejoinder that startled them both. "I think it's a toss-up."

They backed away from each other. Old times, old responses inserted themselves, and Trey blushed.

Luke didn't seem to notice as he turned to his sister. "You okay?"

Frankie squared her shoulders and flipped her long single braid back. "Of course I'm okay."

"Dad says they have to fly George to Bismarck in a helicopter. They say his pulse is a lot stronger now, and they don't have what they need to treat him here."

"See?" Trey offered. "It's a good sign. Things are still working inside that head." He turned to Luke. "I can't believe that Tom Tom. He wasn't more than four or five last time I saw him."

"Wait till you see Beaver."

It was an awkward time, mixing anxiety with what might have been a happy reunion. When Trey said, "It's good to see you, Luke," it sounded almost like a condolence.

Luke clapped a hand on his friend's shoulder. "It's been too long, buddy."

Frankie remembered how inseparable they had once been. Sometimes they had been willing to include George in their exploits. Once in a while Trey's brother had been favored. On the rare occasions when Frankie had been privileged to ride to a game with Luke and Trey, or to sit near them or to be an almost visible part of their crowd, she could hardly see for the stars in her eyes.

"I hear the tables have turned." Trey gave Luke a conspirator's smile. "Your brother's after my sister."

"I suppose you think you owe me a fight."

"Not me."

He glanced at Frankie, but she refused to acknowledge the reference to that foolish time. A stupid moment when the stars had burned out of control. It meant no more now than it had then. In the silence, her rebuff registered, and she felt as though she had scored.

Small victory. Trey dismissed her, just as he had done in the old days, and turned to confide his concerns to Luke. "Lannie needs to be near him now. I hope that's not a problem. I hope you'll make a little space for her."

"With this family, you have to make your own space," Frankie grumbled.

"George would want her near him," Luke said. Frankie got the "back-off" signal as Luke changed the subject. "So you're the sheriff now."

"Just temporarily."

"Chuck Two Hawk is investigating this. I told him George said he was meeting Lannie and, of course, he wants to talk to her."

"We're anxious to talk to him, too," Trey said.

Police Officer Chuck Two Hawk was conducting his investigation near the coffee urn in the hospital staff lounge. It struck Trey that Big Chuck had settled in comfortably, and no hospital staff member was likely to suggest that he move his business elsewhere. No doubt he wanted to be on hand to get Gorgeous George's side of the story as soon as he was able to tell it, and other witnesses seemed to be stopping by in a pretty handy way. It was an enviable way to conduct an investigation. This sure wasn't Denver.

Trey didn't figure to be involved in this case unless it turned out there were non-Indian suspects. Right now he was sticking by Lannie, who'd been pretty damn quiet about just how serious her relationship with George Tracker was until today. On the way to the hospital it had been as if the floodgates had opened. All he'd told her was that there had been an apparent assault, and George had been taken to the hospital—that was all he knew—and suddenly her world had seemed about to collapse. He'd driven her to the hospital because she was too distraught to drive herself.

Two Hawk didn't seem to mind having the whole crew in on his interview with Lannie. Luke and Frankie wanted to hear what she had to say, and Trey was satisfied that she would only have to tell her story once this way. He was sure she didn't know much about the assault. It was hard to put violence and Lannie in the same sentence. He took a chair near hers, while Luke and Frankie sat on the opposite side of the table.

Chuck Two Hawk wasn't much for preliminaries. He got to the point, even though he approached it at an angle. "You guys heard about this on the two-way, right?"

"I heard the call," Trey said. "It sounded like George was hurt pretty bad, so I brought Lannie over because…" He glanced at his sister. "She asked me to."

Because she was in love with the man, which was hard for Trey to imagine. It had nothing to do with the differences between them. There probably weren't very many, really. They both spent a lot of effort trying to please people. Trey remembered George as the life of the party. Race described him as the town drunk. Lannie said he'd changed. Trey had been gone a long time, and he felt like a spectator who'd just missed a big chunk of the show. He'd lost track of the players—one of whom was his sister, who'd never had a real boyfriend.

And now she had to answer the same questions he himself had put to more witnesses than he could count.

"You were with George last night?" Two Hawk began.

"Until about midnight," Lannie said quietly. "He'd asked me to meet him at the Bridge City Steak House, so I did."

Two Hawk turned his little yellow pad to the side and made a note. "What time was that?"

"I got there at about fifteen to seven. George was already there. We had dinner and went to the late show."

"What time did that get out?"

"About eleven."

"Then what did you do?"

"We walked along Main Street, just sort of window-shopping."

"Did you stop in at any of the bars?"

"No."

"Talk to anyone on the street?"

"Only…" Lannie looked to Trey, as if she needed permission or encouragement to go ahead. He felt uncomfortable and thought maybe it was because this spectator role didn't fit him. He couldn't coach, either. She cleared her throat then and continued. "Only my brother, Race. He was with a couple of his friends."

Race. Damn, that kid's mouth would ruin him yet.

"Were they on foot, too?" Two Hawk asked.

"No. They were in Race's pickup. Marty Beecher and some other guy."

"They just stopped to say hello?"

She shook her head. Her thin hands were folded like white linen in her lap, and she stared at them. "Race said something like…that I ought to be getting home. Something stupid like that."

Two Hawk glanced at Trey, who betrayed no hint of the fact that he wished to God he had taken Race up on that beer last night.

The policeman turned back to Lannie. "Did he say anything to George?"

"Just…that he ought to stay away from me or else." Lannie blushed with embarrassment.

Trey didn't like the look he thought Two Hawk was giving her. He had to be thinking that Lannie was too old for her younger brother to be chasing men off for her. But Trey's thoughts quickly came round to the realization that Two Hawk really wasn't looking at her in any way. It was Trey himself who was having trouble. He chafed under the weight of his own feeling of disgust and a long-standing need to distance himself from the effects of his father's "Latimer policy."

"Or what?" Two Hawk prompted.

"He was just being sarcastic. Race and his friends had been drinking, and Race can get pretty obnoxious sometimes," Lannie explained.

"Well, your brother's part Chippewa," Two Hawk said. "Those Chippewas can be tough." He looked to the Trackers, fellow Sioux, for confirmation. Trey had heard such remarks before, even though he knew the basis for the ancient rivalry had gone by the boards long ago. Luke half chuckled, and Frankie refused to respond at all.

Two Hawk continued with his questions. "Was George drinking pretty heavy, too?"

"He wasn't drinking at all. He quit." It was Lannie's turn to look to the Trackers for support. "Weeks— *months ago*—he quit."

"She's right," Frankie supplied.

"You sure could smell it on him," Two Hawk said. "But we'll get that in the medical report. Any threats made?"

"No."

"Did Race get out of the pickup?"

"No. They drove on." She waited until he stopped writing and glanced up at her, signaling for more. "And we sat in my car for a little while, talking. George wasn't worried about Race."

"You been going with George long?"

"Since June eighth."

"Did he take you home last night?"

"No. We've tried to avoid..." She paused, then sighed. "Trouble. I live with my father, you know, and Race. But they'll have to take care of themselves pretty soon. I just put a deposit on an apartment, so I'll be moving. George was pleased when I told him."

Trey had been pleased, too. He had tried to tell their father, calmly at first, that it was long past time Lannie had a life of her own.

"How about Race? Was he pleased?"

"Race was upset because my father was upset."

"Have they let you see George?"

"Yes," Lannie reported softly. "For just a minute."

"You think he might have had a run-in with Race and his friends after you left him?"

"Oh, no." Again she looked at Trey. "No, not Race. He does get himself into a fight occasionally, but not like that. He's fair. He doesn't…" She turned to Frankie, pleading for understanding. "Race would never do a thing like this."

Frankie showed no sign of emotion. She held her head high with a hint of defiance, but she also held her tongue. Trey remembered that look well. Nonnegotiable, it signaled a complete shutout.

"So you went home in your own car, and George…"

"He said he was going home, too. He said he thought we were going to get a storm."

Two Hawk dropped his black, government issue ballpoint pen on the yellow pad, leaned back in his chair and spoke to Trey. "The Mobridge police found his pickup parked on Main Street, probably right where he left it last night. He must have hooked up with somebody—" he glanced at Lannie "—after you left him."

"He talked about spending time with Luke," she said. "He said Luke and his wife were leaving for Germany in a day or two, and he said he only had a little bit of time to make up for a lot that he'd lost with his brother." The information was given for Luke's benefit, but Luke was all military man. His reaction was hard to read. Lannie wasn't good at pushing, but, on behalf of George, she sought to make an impression on Luke. "He's been going to AA meetings. Did you know that?" she pressed.

Frankie said, "Sure, we knew," at the same time Luke was saying, "No."

"Well, I guess he got sidetracked," Two Hawk said. He would let them compare notes on the Gorgeous George they all knew and loved on their own time. All he needed were witnesses and suspects.

He turned to Trey. "I'll have to talk to your brother." Trey nodded. "And his friends."

"Is that my department? His friends?"

"Do you know Beecher?" Two Hawk asked.

"I know who he is."

"See what you can get out of him. Non-Indians get real touchy sometimes about being questioned by Indian cops." He pushed himself away from the table with one hand while he pocketed his notes with the other. "Well, you know how that is."

"Sure," Trey said. "But a cop's a cop, Chuck."

"Not around here. Here we've got two sets of cops for two sets of people." Two Hawk reached back to tuck his shirt into his pants as he stood. Everyone else gratefully took the cue. "Guess I'd better get going on what we've got so far." He turned to Luke. "They're flying George to Bismarck, right? Will you be around for a while?"

"I can get an emergency extension, but I don't know for how long."

"Call me right away if there are any changes. I want to arrest somebody for this."

It was a sentiment Trey understood. A cop *was* a cop, and arresting a solid suspect was the best vindication any officer had to offer. But Trey figured that Frankie and Luke took the promise with a grain of salt as they led the way out the door. Lannie followed them, and Trey held the door, bringing up the rear. He felt a little dazed. Part of him had already asserted himself as a lawman again, while the other part was running to catch up, shouting, *Hold on a minute, you jerk. This is your brother they're talking about.*

"Sheriff?"

Trey's reaction was delayed by the fact that he hadn't gotten used to his title, but Two Hawk must have thought he was being ignored.

"Wait up, Latimer."

Trey turned, and Two Hawk indicated with a jerk of his chin that he should stay. Trey wasn't ready for a conference right now, but he stepped back and closed the door.

Two Hawk stood like a mountain, arms akimbo. "If Tracker dies, it becomes a federal case. The FBI takes over. That tips everything in the other direction. Indians don't like being questioned by FBI, so they clam up."

"So then we're both out of it." In his old job, he would have been out of it the minute a relative was involved. In Corson County it wouldn't be so easy. Everybody seemed to be connected to everybody else in one way or another.

"Depends."

"On whether my brother's a suspect?"

Two Hawk shrugged. "You seem like a good cop."

"I got a medical retirement, Chuck. This job's only temporary. And I'm hoping George Tracker regains consciousness real soon and tells us who did this to him."

"No matter who it was?"

"Right. No matter who it was." Trey folded his arms across his chest. "Besides, it isn't just a question of who, but where. George was found on Indian land, which is your jurisdiction, and in Corson County, which is mine. But now we've got his pickup in Mobridge, which is Walworth County. So we don't know where all this happened."

"Maybe Race knows," Two Hawk said, and Trey had no answer for that. "I hope he isn't gonna get touchy about being questioned by a B.I.A. cop. I might have to remind him of something he don't much like hearing." Trey waited for Two Hawk to make a point that could easily have gone without saying. "That he's an Indian."

"You do your job, Chuck. I'll check Beecher out and get back to you later." He started for the door, but there was something else he wanted understood, and Two Hawk was as good a sounding board as he was likely to get right now. "I played basketball with George and Luke," he told the policeman. It was just for the record. *Any*body's record. "Luke was my best friend."

"How many brothers you got?"

"One." Race could be obnoxious sometimes, just as Lannie had said. But Trey pictured that endearing grin. "One brother."

"If the FBI steps in, we become friendly local law enforcement. We give them whatever we've got, and then they do things their way."

"Yeah." Two Hawk was saying they could both be off the hook. "I know how that goes." Red tape, Frankie would call it.

"I'll call you if I need you for anything else."

They left the staff lounge together, and Two Hawk went on his way. Trey wasn't sure what he should do next. He was there as a friend, not a cop. No one acknowledged him as he took what he thought would be an inoffensive position on the fringe of the Tracker family, maybe one step up from bystander. He hoped someone would include him somehow—ask him for a favor or maybe some kind of an opinion.

He looked at Frankie, hoping she would remember that he'd had something to offer a little while ago. But in the few minutes he'd spent with Two Hawk, the Trackers had closed ranks, and Trey was on the outside looking in. His best friend glanced through him. The beautiful woman he'd comforted earlier wouldn't spare him a glimpse of her dark eyes.

"I'm going to ride to the hospital with the Trackers," Lannie told him. The plan came as a surprise. "They're taking two outfits, so Luke says there's room for me. George's mother is at home, so we're going to stop there."

Trey felt as though he were looking at Lannie through a window. Wasn't Race her brother, too? She had been included in the Tracker group, while suddenly he might have been sitting on another planet.

The chill-out made him bristle. "How'll you get back?"

"I'll worry about that later."

The elder George Tracker emerged from the hinterlands of hospital corridors. "They're ready to go," he announced. "I've signed all their papers."

Impulsively, Trey stepped forward. "Mr. Tracker?" The old man didn't recognize him. "Trey Latimer. I used to—"

"Trey." George offered a gentle Indian-style handshake. "Good to see you. You been gone a long time." He perused Trey's face in a frank way, as only the young and the elderly were wont to do. "Got a little age on you."

"City living can do that to a country boy." George nodded. Trey added quickly, "I've seen a lot of this kind of injury, Mr. Tracker. It looks bad, I know, but it can turn around anytime."

The people surrounding him didn't seem to be buying any of his good intentions. Except maybe the old man, who patted Trey's elbow and nodded wearily. Trey had always envied Luke his big, boisterous family. It had been more fun to help the Trackers haul bales in the summer than it was to hang around construction sites with his own father and get paid to listen to him preach against everything from Democrats to Ford pickups. He remembered wishing the Trackers would adopt him and

Luke telling him there might be room in the younger boys' bed if he didn't mind Beaver's smelly feet and Tom Tom's jabbering in his sleep.

Trey stood there watching them leave, taking his sister with them. He'd been gone a long time. In the space of thirteen years he'd been through a career and a marriage. He tried to remember why, of all the places he could have chosen to start over, he'd come back to South Dakota. There was a time in a young man's life when he couldn't get far enough away, but the road had a way of circling back. Trey wasn't sure why. He only knew he wanted to be heading up to Bismarck with the Tracker family, who knew how to pull together.

And he wished he'd never gotten himself into this sheriff's job.

Chapter 3

Trey sympathized with the Trackers, but when the Bureau of Indian Affairs police arrested his brother, he acted on instinct. Blood was thicker than locker room sweat and victory party beer. Race had made some remarks, sure, but that didn't mean he had tried to kill George Tracker. There wasn't enough evidence to hold the kid on an assault charge. Couldn't be. Trey himself had talked to Marty Beecher, who'd said that Race was just kidding around, looking for a little scrap. Stupid, Trey acknowledged. He didn't know what Race was trying to prove, but he knew Lannie was right. Fighting was a Saturday-night sport around here, but going in for the kill wasn't part of Race's game.

A sign along the two-lane highway proclaimed that Trey was entering North Dakota. He was still on the reservation, and, in that respect, the state line meant nothing. Standing Rock Sioux Reservation had been there first. The countryside changed gradually as he drove north. Fewer square-topped buttes and more rolling hills. But the endless sea of grass, yellowing now in the hot August sun, rolled across all the lines people used to define the places they named or claimed.

Trey felt funny about storming the Indian police station in search of his brother. Trey had grown up with the understanding that there were entities like the Indian police, Indian hospitals and Indian housing. He had always had mixed feelings about them. They weren't exactly closed to him, but they weren't for his use. They were places where a white kid might venture with an Indian friend, or maybe in search of him. But he'd never gone looking for his brother in any of those places, even though, technically, his brother was an Indian.

He remembered the day his father had brought the dark-eyed little boy into the house and announced that he would be living there. Nothing was said about Race's mother. Lannie and Trey had heard their parents argue in the night. Their frail mother would cry and hiss an occasional accusation about Phillip's "girlfriends," and he would tell her to leave him alone. Trey didn't know how Lannie had handled it, but he'd taken to covering his head with a pillow and fashioning a little tunnel in front of his mouth so he could breathe.

After Race came, there were no more arguments. Trey remembered his mother's wounded looks and the way she had retreated into her private bedroom while the rest of the family carried on their lives in hushed tones. Her death had simply completed her retreat. But it was she who had told Trey that Race was Phillip's son.

Surprisingly, Trey had felt relieved. That explained

the mystery. He had wanted a brother, and even though Race, six years his junior, was too young to be a real buddy, Trey had figured he would grow. He'd told Lannie the news. Indignantly, she had questioned their father. Race had been with them for two years by that time, and Lannie had become the little mother. Was Race a Latimer? While Phillip begrudged the boy his name, his stalwart, unemotional sense of duty prevented him from denying his paternity. Legally, Race became a Latimer. Race's mother was rarely discussed, and although Phillip acknowledged that Race was "part Indian," he never talked about that part. As far as Trey knew, Race never asked about it.

The B.I.A. police were headquartered in the agency town of Fort Yates, which was shored up by dikes to keep the mighty Missouri River from swallowing it up. Trey turned his pickup at the causeway that traversed the river's backwater and tethered the town to the highway like an asphalt mooring. It was the picture of a town literally hanging by a thread against the encroachment of a heavily dammed river. Fort Yates had been the site of the Standing Rock Sioux Agency since before the turn of the century, and it was from this site that Indian policemen had been dispatched in 1890 to arrest Sitting Bull.

Trey knew some of the history, but he knew little of Indian law and justice. It was all based on treaty rights. The fact that the county sheriff and the Indian police were cross-deputized had seemed like a courtesy when he'd accepted the badge. Now he hoped it wouldn't interfere with his present mission, which was simply to do what he could to get his brother out of jail.

It looked as though their father had beaten him to it. The big silver-and-blue road hog Phillip Latimer called a pickup was parked next to the curb near the Department of Law and Order sign. Trey could just see the old man trying to throw his weight around in a place where nobody was likely to give a damn who Phillip Latimer was. Trey's need to avoid the man sat on his brain's back burner, simmering slowly. But he had come back home of his own accord, and there were certain things he would have to deal with.

He wondered when the old man would finally have the heart attack he'd been angling for all these years. His flaming red face and the vessels bulging in his slick forehead were not a good sign. He was toe-to-toe with Two Hawk, standing behind the dispatcher's station, and Big Chuck was holding his ground. Phillip Latimer's proverbial weight was probably the least of Two Hawk's worries.

When he finally noticed Trey, Phillip threw up his hands and made his way around the reception desk and into the hallway, grumbling, "This is ridiculous. Can't you do something about this?"

Trey acknowledged Two Hawk with a nod. The policeman returned the greeting in kind and proceeded with some business he had with the dispatcher. Meanwhile, Trey sidestepped his father, who was coming at him like a bulldozer. "I don't know," he said, his voice a calm counterpoint. "I'll have to find out what's going on."

"They're holding your brother. That's what's going on." Phillip maneuvered around Trey so he could see the people in the office area, who were doing their best to ignore him. He wanted to be sure they could overhear his every word. "They're trying to pin this Tracker thing on him."

"Have you called Marvin Kelly? He's still your attorney, isn't he?"

"Hell, I don't need an attorney. These guys have overstepped their bounds here. They can't hold him."

"They can if they think they've got something on him."

"Let me tell you something, Trey. This isn't Denver. These are Indian police. If anybody's gonna arrest a Latimer—"

Two Hawk appeared in the doorway. "Got some news for you, Mr. Latimer. Your son's an enrolled member of the Turtle Mountain Chippewa. We checked it out, just to be sure."

"Somebody's lying." Phillip postured with his hands at his hips. He glared at Two Hawk, Trey, even the dispatcher. Trey looked away in disgust.

Phillip expounded, "His mother left him with me when he wasn't much more than a baby. She didn't do a damn thing for him, and I sure as hell never enrolled him with any Turtle Mountain Chippewa." He rolled out the last words as if they were overblown and ludicrous.

"Well, somebody did. And we've got witnesses who say that Race made some pretty strong threats. Right now, he's the best suspect we've got." Two Hawk snatched a phone off the desk next to the door and held it up like an offering. "So you get your lawyer in here and see what the judge says about whether we hold him. I'm thinking George might just come to anytime and give us all we need."

"You can't hold him on what you've got," Trey said matter-of-factly.

"We've got him now, though." Two Hawk set the phone down and made Phillip another offer. "You want to see him? I can sure let you see him." He chuckled. "He's about as mad as you are, only he's twice as mean."

"I'll see him soon enough when he gets home."

It was Phillip Latimer's bottom line. Trey wanted
to rail at him for it, but railing at his father was a thing
he did only in his head. Outwardly he spared only
quiet disgust.

"Call Kelly. You can do that much." He could not
look at the man now. Instead, he turned to Two Hawk.
"I'm here to see him, Chuck."

The policeman led him through the pale green and
white maze of locks and gates to the cell containing his
disgruntled brother. Trey figured the loss of his cowboy
hat and his tooled belt with the big silver probably
bothered Race the most. The young man came up off
the bunk like a shot when he saw his brother, and Trey
wished he could say that he'd come to the rescue.
Barring that, at least for the moment, maybe he could
lift the kid's spirits.

"If I didn't know better, I'd say you guys had caught
yourselves a gen-u-ine outlaw, Chuck." Race cocked his
chin and made a fist. Trey turned to his brother and
offered a quick sign of surrender. "But I do know better.
We'll get you out of here as soon as we can."

"You and who? The cavalry?" Race countered.
Two Hawk laughed heartily as he unlocked Race's
cell and let Trey in. "Did you know I had an enroll-
ment number?"

"The subject never came up." They'd never done any
hugging. Not amongst the Latimer men. Trey wished
that he could do it now, do it naturally, the way some
men did. He shook his head and stuck his hands in the
back pockets of his jeans. "I don't know much about it,
Race. I suppose your mother just filled out some papers."

"Before or after she dumped me on the old man's
doorstep?" Race glanced past Trey, past the cell bars at

the empty hallway. "Where is he, anyway? I called and told Lannie—"

"He's, uh…getting hold of a lawyer, which is what you really need most right now."

"I really need cigarettes." Trey had anticipated that need, and Race accepted the fresh pack gratefully. "I'm surprised to see you."

"Lannie called me."

"And you called your buddy Tracker, right?" Race offered Trey the first cigarette from the pack. "Luke must be chomping at the bit to have it out with me right about now."

"I'm not asking you whether you had anything to do with this, Race. This is Two Hawk's arrest. Not mine." Trey didn't want the cigarette, but he took it anyway. Race lit it and his own with the same match. It was something shared, and the smoke smelled better than jailhouse disinfectant and stagnant air.

"But anything I say to a cop can be used against me," Race concluded on the tail of a stream of smoke.

"That's right." Trey's instincts were battling for the floor. *You have the right to remain silent. You have the right to expect your brother to back you, no matter what.* He lifted one hand in frustration. "Look, I'm not a cop anymore. I came home for some peace and quiet, you know?" Race didn't know. Why would he know? *How* would he know? "I just want to raise a few good horses and watch the sun rise and set. This sheriff's badge is a temporary thing."

"Does that mean you're not serious about it?"

"No. It just means… Damn it, Race, you could have stayed out of trouble until after they elected somebody else."

Race stared coldly, and Trey tried to wave the chill away. "I'm not accusing you. If I thought you had anything to do with this, I'd be the first to—"

To what? Race's eyes demanded.

Trey sighed. "But I don't. I just wish you'd left Lannie alone."

"*Gorgeous* George." Race expressed his disbelief with a slow shake of his head. "What a joke that is. You've been gone a long time, Trey. George Tracker got kicked out of the army for raising hell, and he's probably—" He glanced at the Spartan cot, then at the toilet without a seat. "Hell, I'm probably occupying his favorite accommodations."

"You want to trade places with him?"

"I didn't put him there."

"He still hasn't regained consciousness."

"I'm sorry to hear that." Race took a long pull on his cigarette as he moved toward the cell bars. He sent a lungful of smoke into the passageway beyond them. "But I didn't knock him out. I admit I did tell him to stay away from Lannie. Later on, I saw him walking back to his pickup, and I had a little talk with him. And we sorta got into it, but it was nothing. I didn't even hit him."

Trey scowled. "I talked to Marty Beecher. He didn't say anything about running into George a second time."

"Marty was in the Silver Dollar. Nick Zahn was with me, but he figured it was between me and Tracker, so he went back inside."

Bad timing on Zahn's part. "So Nick is one of the witnesses Two Hawk was talking about."

"I guess that's why they've got me in here. But nobody saw me hit him."

Great.

"Because I didn't hit him," Race said.

"What did you do? Shove him around?"

"Yeah, I shoved him, and he shoved back." Race closed his free hand around one of the bars as he watched his brother imagine each move and anticipate the next.

Who are you, brother? Trey wondered.

Race stared past the bars again. "Then he walked away."

"Were you drunk?"

"I'd had a few beers. I wasn't drunk."

"How about George? They didn't find much alcohol in his blood."

"He was sober when I saw him." Pushing himself away from the bars, Race turned, and the expression in his eyes softened. "Listen, I don't want to see the guy dead. I just don't want to see him hanging around my sister. She's completely different from him. She's—"

"Maybe she's making a difference in his life, and maybe he can do the same for her." Race snorted, and Trey grabbed his arm. "People change, Race. So maybe the rest of us should mind our own damn business."

"Yeah, right." Race pulled away. "It sounds to me like somebody went to a whole lot of trouble to put George Tracker out of commission." His dark eyes burned with some quickened fervor even as he backed away, as though Trey's hand on his arm had been an offense. "I'd never go that far. I don't know why I'd expect you to know that. Hell, I was only thirteen when you left here. You don't know anything about me."

"I know you're my brother. And I know they can't hold you here on what they've got. But if he dies, Race…"

The fervor died, leaving two coal-black voids in Race's face. He spoke bitterly. "If he dies, I hope all you cops can find his killer."

"I do, too."

When Marvin Kelly showed up, Trey could've sworn he heard a bugler somewhere sounding the charge. Trey had the feeling Kelly could keep every promise he made, the first being, "I'll have you out of here in no time."

Those words coming out of a lawyer's mouth made his gut roil automatically. He had to keep reminding himself that the shoe was on the other foot. He figured, on the basis of the evidence Two Hawk had, that "no time" would probably mean within the hour. He left Race with his attorney, but he was planning to hang around the reception area to see how it all turned out.

That was where he ran into Frankie.

"What are you doing here?" he asked. He'd been thinking about calling Luke, hoping for a reception warm enough to leave the door open for some other overture. Like maybe calling Frankie.

"I heard they'd arrested somebody for beating up my brother, so I stopped in to check it out." She indicated the front desk with a brief glance. The desk was unmanned at the moment, but Two Hawk was a few steps away, sorting through the files in the top drawer of a tall cabinet. "And since I've checked it out, I don't need to ask why you're here," she said flatly.

His brother wasn't the one he wanted to talk with her about. "How's George?"

"The same." She stood there like an ice sculpture and offered a bit of news she seemed to think would put her one up on him. "They say there's brain activity."

"That's good." Her shoulders sagged a little then, as though the starch in them were wilting. "Really, that's good." He wanted to coax those shoulders back up.

"Except they won't tell us why he doesn't come out of it," she admitted quietly.

"They don't know. I know sometimes it seems like they don't want to tell you everything, but with something like this, the doctors are guessing, too." He nodded toward the door. "Want to get some air?" Without waiting for an answer, he pushed the door open and held it for her as he donned his nearly broken-in straw cowboy hat.

"What does that mean—brain activity?" she asked, taking the lead. "Does it mean he knows what's going on, but he can't make his body move? Is he trapped inside his own head?"

"It means his brain is alive."

"Well, could he be paralyzed? Could he be…" She turned to him as she stepped into the tree-mottled sunlight. He let the door close behind him. "Why am I asking you?"

It was a good question. There had been a time when she'd asked him all kinds of good questions, and when he'd run out of answers, he'd called her a pest. Not so now. The only thing pesky about those big black eyes was the fact that they'd changed so little, when the rest of her, gone from girl to woman, had changed so much.

"I wish I had some answers for you, Frankie. Is he up at Bismarck Hospital?"

"Yes, for now. Once they've done all they can up there, they'll probably move him down here to PHS if he's still…like that."

He knew that PHS was still the popular term for the Fort Yates hospital, even though it was no longer *Public* but *Indian* Health Service. Government agencies kept busy by reorganizing.

Her tone turned accusatory. "You're going to get him off, aren't you?"

"Who, Race?" Trey sighed as he surveyed the quiet street. Directly on the opposite side, a row of yellow school buses stood behind a chain-link fence, waiting for the end of summer. "Race didn't do it."

"You know what?" she began impatiently. "Race's reputation is just about a match for George's. Except that George never hurt anybody but himself."

Trey glanced over his shoulder at the south end of the building, where he'd met with his brother. "Race just pointed out to me that I don't know much about his reputation. Which is true. I've been gone a long time, and I haven't…" He shook his head. "Race didn't do it. That much I do know."

"What if he did? What if George wakes up and says he did?"

"Then the courts decide."

"The courts, the courts." Frankie folded her arms beneath her breasts, unconsciously emphasizing that soft-looking part of her otherwise boyishly slender body. "Race Latimer won't serve one day, and you know it. You Latimers have always been able to do as you damn well please. You don't care."

"Of course I care. Luke and George are my—"

"Friends?" Her eyes flashed as she bit out, "Sure. Then why isn't George good enough to go out with your sister?"

"I never said—"

"Your brother did. Who does he think he is? Your sister ought to be able to take care of herself."

"That's true."

She unfolded her arms and held them stiffly by her

sides as she assessed him frankly—he wasn't sure what she was looking for. A motive for his willingness to agree with her, maybe. For a moment she held his attention with a mesmerizing gaze, but he found her eyes too compelling. He shifted his own gaze to her sleek black hair, caught up in a French braid and glinting in the sunlight. He thought about the many ways he'd seen her wear her hair. Always long. Always straight and shiny.

But she was still thinking of his brother. "He didn't do it alone, either. I want them to find out who else..."

"Frankie." She started to walk away, but he caught her arm. She pulled away, much the way Race had, and backed into a curbside phone booth.

"Frankie, listen. It doesn't matter whether the whole town of Mobridge gets put away for this. That isn't going to do George any good now."

She glanced away. "That's...that's what my father says, too."

Thank God for an old man's wisdom. "Let the police worry about getting the guy who's responsible."

"I think they've got him." Caught between him and the drive-up phone booth, she challenged the one with a hot stare while she tapped the other with the side of her fist. "But I think you'll make them let him go."

Trey figured that if he had been the phone booth, the taps would have been given more force.

"I can't make them do anything. They'll do what's right." One last whack on the metal booth accompanied one good scowl. The nickname "Gorgeous" had gone to the wrong Tracker—a thought that brought Trey's good sense around. "Frankie, I'd really like to go up and see George."

"Nobody's stopping you." She lifted one bare

shoulder. "Luke's usually there, but he probably won't be much longer."

"Uncle Sam wants him back, huh?" He watched her tuck a stray wisp of hair behind her ear. "Listen, I don't know what to say about Race. He—"

The answer came from behind.

"You don't have to say anything about Race." They both turned sharply. The cowboy hat and belt had been restored, and Race was smiling. "Your brother Race is just passing through. Kelly said the magic words, and I promised not to go anywhere for a while. You cops are gonna have to come up with something more convincing."

Joining them at the curb, Race turned to Frankie. "I didn't work your brother over, and I'm sorry he's in tough shape. I didn't think he was right for Lannie. I still don't."

Trey cast a glance heavenward and sighed. Frankie's eyes narrowed, but she offered no comment. Race turned on his heel and cut across the grass, muttering, "Hell with it. Let her do what she wants."

"You need a ride?" Trey called out.

"Kelly's going my way."

Race was headed for the back of the building, where Kelly's car was undoubtedly parked. Trey chided himself for feeling relieved. Race was playing it especially bullheaded at the moment and he didn't want to spend an hour on the road with him, no matter how much Race needed a friend.

"You wouldn't believe the change in George lately," Frankie said. Trey turned, looking at her quizzically. "Since he started going with your sister." Frankie glanced away and confided, almost in awe of the very thought, "She sits beside his bed by the hour and holds his hand."

Trey had to admit that it was hard to imagine George holding hands with Lannie. When they were kids, George had often been permitted to tag along after Luke, but generally they'd drawn the line there. Race was just a kid, even younger than Frankie, who was a kid *and* a girl. George was fun to have around. Lannie was never part of any of it. She was beyond having fun.

"Strange match," Trey said.

"Maybe so, but she's sticking by him."

"That counts for a lot." He shoved his hands into his pockets and glanced up the street. He knew that the blue hatchback parked in front of his pickup was hers, because he'd made it his business to know. "Have you been up to the hospital today?"

"I was on my way."

"Can I give you a lift? You could leave your car here, pick it up on the way back."

"No." She dug her keys out of her pocket as if his offer were a signal to take to the highway. "I like having my own wheels under me."

"The rest of the world is promoting the share-a-ride concept." He smiled and pushed his straw hat back like a befuddled cowpoke. "Guess I forgot I was back in the Dakotas."

She shook her head, uncharmed. "Thanks for the offer."

He stood there watching her get into her car, which really made her nervous. Half the time the stupid thing wouldn't start. She was trying to think up a good remark in case this turned out to be one of those times when the sweet little put-put started in. Ah. She smiled at him, gave a quick wave and made a U-turn right there in front of the police station. She could hear Trey laughing, but she resisted giving him a last look. She didn't know what was so funny about getting yourself headed in the right direction.

The blue hatchback ran okay for about fifteen miles. Then it died. Frankie coasted over to the side of the road, got out and took a moment just to glower at the stupid piece of junk. Then she cursed it, along with all its foreign-built relatives, as she flung the door shut. She was so angry, she broke a nail on the stupid hood latch. She'd seen that damn red pickup in her rearview mirror several miles back. He'd probably dropped behind just so he could make a big appearance when she broke down.

She didn't know what she was looking for under the hood, but she figured she ought to be busy with something when he pulled over. *If* he pulled over. She could hear him coming.

He'd damn well better pull over.

"Taking a rest?" he asked after parking his pickup in front of the car.

"It died." She emerged from the mechanical maze, prepared to face a smirk. "Obviously."

"I doubt if it's time to bury it." He stuck his head under the hood and jiggled a few things. "Did it just quit on you?"

"It sputtered a little first." It was amazing how long and tapered his back looked from this angle. She folded her arms and jerked her head to the other side. It was even more amazing that she would notice a thing like that.

"Gas filter, maybe."

Of course he would have the answer she didn't. She wished she could tell him the gas filter had just been changed, but it wouldn't matter. She would still have to accept the ride he'd offered her earlier.

"I have a tow chain."

This offer was above and beyond the first, but the cocky smile was still there. "Leave the damn thing for the vultures," she clipped.

"You won't have any tires left."

She had the pleasure of slamming the hood down. "They're my tires."

"I don't mind towing the car. We'll leave it in Cannon Ball." She glanced up the road as if she might see the town off in the distance, even though she knew it was another five miles. "I happen to be going your way, Frankie."

She turned and looked back down the road. The hot wind lifted the hair that had strayed around her temples from her braid. He happened to be a lot of things she didn't like right now—lawman, brother to a creep, son of a wealthy white businessman who was the father of a creep. Do-gooder. Right now, because she needed help, his willingness to do his good turn rankled her pride the most. That and the fact that she kept catching herself feeling fluttery when she looked at him. Foolishness, all of it.

She told herself to grow up and watched the road for a full minute. Finally, she grumbled, "I don't see too many other choices."

"Guess I win by default."

They left the car at the trailer house gas station just outside Cannon Ball. From there, it was another fifty miles, which was a long way for Frankie to avoid looking at the driver. And, of course, he wanted to be chatting the whole time.

"I hear you're a teacher now. How do you like teaching?"

"It's good."

"Little kids, big kids—what?"

"Second grade."

There was a pause, and then a hint of melancholia in his voice. "My daughter's going to be in second grade this year."

"Your daughter?" Frankie tried to imagine a small, feminine version of Trey. Probably towheaded, knobby-kneed, big round blue eyes. The voice of a father missing his child came unexpectedly, and it tapped into her special reserve of sympathy.

"Her name's Tricia. Her mother and I split up three years ago. They moved to Colorado Springs, so she'll be starting in a new school." He dropped his hand over the gearshift and looked across the cab at her. "Is that pretty hard on a kid her age?"

"It depends on how outgoing she is." Those sad gray eyes revealed too much of him, she thought. He ought to hide them behind dark glasses. "Do you see her much?"

"She'll be spending the summer with me next year. She loves horses. By next summer I should have the house fixed up a little nicer, and we'll have a few colts and some kittens in the barn. And I promised her ducks." His eyes brightened, and there were spokes at the corners when he cracked half a smile. "Baby ducks."

"Sounds like fun." And a subject to be avoided if she were going to bear in mind that he was closely related to a creep. "It's kind of a surprise, you moving back here and getting into ranching."

"I had to make some changes."

"So you came back to South Dakota and took a job as a sheriff? You must not have had too many choices, either."

Even the sound of his chuckle was disarming. "Thinking too hard gives me a headache these days. I decided to go with the flow, and I kinda washed up on the banks of the Missouri."

"You're pretty young to be washed up," she asserted.

"That's what I figured." He downshifted for a hill. "I used to hate the quiet out here. The way you can drive all morning and pass maybe ten cars."

"You and Luke both."

"Luke really likes the army, doesn't he? I gave him a bad time about it when he first enlisted. I was looking for excitement, and I thought the army sounded pretty much like South Dakota. Same old drab green and brown."

"Did you find excitement in Denver?"

"Yeah. I found it." The pickup nosed over the rise, and the river stretched out below them. A scattering of black baldy cows grazed in the sun. "This little place I bought... You know the old Bowker place?"

She nodded. "It's out in the sticks."

He laughed. "Out in the sticks, she says. You guys live—"

"Our place is right near the highway." Everybody knew that highway access made all the difference.

"Well, I'm twenty-five minutes from Mobridge, but you'd never know you were that close to a town out there."

Times and Trey Latimer had certainly changed if that was the way he wanted it. "Had enough excitement?"

"No. I'm just looking for a different kind these days." He stuck his elbow out the window, propping his forearm on the door, and guided the steering wheel into his right hand with a little help from his left. "Is it exciting to be a teacher?"

"Seven-year-olds can really keep it lively."

He had nice hands. She imagined the wedding band he must have worn at one time and wondered why he hadn't replaced it with a big, chunky onyx or flashy Black Hills gold.

"I thought you'd have children of your own by now," he said.

"Haven't had time." She decided she ought to be able to wonder aloud, if he could. "Was your wife pretty?" She enjoyed his look of surprise. "I'll bet she was kind of ruffly and pink, wasn't she?"

"Pink?" He raised his brow, as if he had to think that one over. "If Connie had a color, I guess it was kind of creamy."

"Same difference. Kind of like your sister." He laughed, and she injected, "But pretty." And then he stared, and she wanted to bite her tongue. "I didn't mean it that way," she said quietly.

"Lannie isn't pretty. But she's beautiful." He shrugged. "*I* think."

"I think—" she couldn't help smiling "—that *one* beautiful person is like a saving grace in a family."

"Right." He returned a cocky grin. "That's why you guys were blessed with the Gorgeous One."

It was Frankie's turn for a shrug. "Pink and creamy is okay, but it doesn't suit *everybody.*"

"Doesn't do a thing for me." He glanced her way, catching her chewing on the nail she'd broken on the hood latch. She shoved her hand between her denim-clad knees, and another smile dawned in his eyes. "Anymore."

Yeah, right. Pretty golden men liked pretty pink women.

But he had a flaw that gave his physical beauty a new raw edge, and she wondered about it. "You had to have some kind of surgery on your head, didn't you?"

"Yep." He touched the scar that arrowed above his

right eyebrow. "They did some fancy reconstruction on me. Put in a metal plate where there used to be bone."

"Does it hurt?"

"Sometimes, yeah."

"George's skull is fractured, they said." He took his hand away, and she studied the thin ridge of puckered flesh that attested to the violence that had been done to him. It was so ironic that he should have this in common with George. She insisted, "I know it wasn't just a fist fight."

"No," he said quietly. "Sure doesn't sound like it."

"Luke has to leave in a few days unless—" It was her second greatest fear, and she kept thinking she'd better not say it, in case saying might make it so. When she did, she said it softly. "You know, unless George dies or something."

His eyes offered her the same tenderness he'd given her at the hospital, and she had a terrible urge to lean against him again, just for a moment. But she swept the urge away with a change of focus.

"He's really crazy about your sister, you know. I told him she didn't seem like his type. Well, anyone can see how prim and proper she is. But he said I couldn't be picking out women for him, because obviously I didn't know anything about his type." Smiling, she spoke fondly. "She's really quiet, but she's nice."

"Unlike her brothers?" Trey chided. Frankie didn't object. "Maybe George doesn't have a type. Maybe he just knows a good thing when he sees one."

"Yeah. Unlike Lannie's brothers."

"What are we talking about here?" Indignant now, he didn't seem to know whether to keep his eyes on the road or try to stare her down. "Are we talking about Race's bad manners? Or mine?"

"Nobody's blaming you for anything. Not unless you get that hotheaded brother of yours off without—"

"I'm not talking about that." She waited. "I'm talking about the night of the Homecoming party. I remember that night, too. You were wearing a red blouse and a very…nice black skirt."

She raised her left eyebrow, recalling the skirt she'd never had the nerve to wear again.

"See?" he said. "I haven't forgotten."

It might have been better if he had left the memory to her. She affected a casual shrug. "You said you'd give me a ride home."

"Yeah, I know. All of a sudden you didn't seem like such a kid anymore."

"And for about two minutes, you didn't seem like such a big, dumb redneck."

"Two minutes?" He shook his head in mock amazement, but his eyes were, blessedly, on the road. "I could've sworn I was on your good side longer than that."

"You always did give yourself more credit than you deserved," she muttered as she watched the pickup's hood lap up bits of yellow line.

"I was sorry you were so young. And sorry I was so…"

"Old?"

He laughed. "Yeah. Old. But fairly nice. I ended up being fairly nice, didn't I?"

"Again, more credit than you deserve." And it bothered her that she was willing to give him that much and then some.

Abruptly, she changed the subject. "Were you good at your job?"

The change threw him off balance, which was the way she liked it. She enjoyed evoking that puzzled look. "I really want to know. Were you a good cop?"

"Yeah, I was good."

"Do you miss it?"

"Sometimes." He thought about it for a moment. "I like being right there when bad guys get caught."

"There are all kinds of bad guys," she said. "And most of them don't get caught."

His double take was penetrating, but she meant no indictment against him this time. He bore a terrible scar, and he'd said nothing to her of the assault on *his* head. Only that it had happened. Under the golden skin and the sun-kissed hair, he knew how it felt. Maybe that spilling of blood had made all the difference.

"Some of them do," he assured her.

"Even so," she said with a sigh, "I think they out-number us."

Chapter 4

Frankie felt weird watching Lannie massage George's feet. It was like peeking into somebody's bedroom window. She tried to get interested in the magazine lying open on her lap, but the article on picky eaters wasn't as disgustingly fascinating as the way Lannie's long, thin fingers stroked the feet that had been molded by cowboy boots. The sharply tapered bunch of toes twitched a little when Lannie pressed her thumbs into George's pronounced arches.

Frankie wondered if they'd ever slept together.

Dwa-lay, what a naughty thought! Frankie snapped the magazine up to her face again and tried to concentrate on the list of suggestions for tempting kids to eat raw vegetables. Heck, she'd tried raw vegetables last year using the Follow Through Program money. The kids had wanted to feed the celery to Barney, the second-grade's rabbit.

Maybe this year she'd ask for a baby duck.

Maybe not. The kids would probably pet it to death. Stroke off all the fuzz. Make it look like a bare, skinny…foot.

George sure had small feet for a man his size.

The magazine said that kids should never wear hand-me-down shoes. Frankie wondered whether the editors had ever tried to keep ten growing children clothed and fed. One pair of boots a year, and sometimes George's one pair was inherited from Luke. He wouldn't say anything when they got too small. He'd worn them until they pinched so bad he couldn't help limping, but he had managed to turn the limp into a bowlegged swagger so their mother wouldn't make him wear tennis shoes. Gorgeous George hated tennis shoes, and he had the boot-shaped feet to prove it.

And here was Lannie Latimer, making this big production, but she wouldn't know anything about hand-me-downs, either. Who was *she* to rub George's feet?

"You don't really think he can feel that, do you?" Frankie demanded. She tossed the magazine on the floor beside her chair.

"I don't know, but it can't hurt to try. When my brother was in the hospital…" Lannie glanced at Frankie. "My brother Trey. He got shot when he was working as a policeman out in—"

"He told me about it." Did Lannie think she didn't know which brother? It felt like a small triumph over this woman who had taken over *her* brother that Frankie had had the story from Trey himself. To prove it she said, "He has a metal plate in his head."

"Yes. He doesn't often talk about it." Lannie went back to her massaging. "Anyway, when he was lying there like this, and we didn't know what was going to happen, the only thing I could think about was, how can I let him know I'm here?"

"So you fooled around with his feet?" It was something Frankie didn't really want to imagine. Lannie's pale, skinny hands on Trey's feet.

"No, but I held his hands and talked to him."

"Shouldn't his wife have been the one doing that?" Frankie knew it was a perverse question. Deliciously so.

"They had already split up before it happened. Of course, she was terribly concerned about him, but it was difficult for her. She didn't know whether she should even be there, but their little girl didn't understand what had happened to her daddy. His head was bandaged. We couldn't see his eyes. He was a mess."

Surprisingly, Frankie didn't like hearing about the "concerned" wife, either, but she'd brought it up.

"So you held his hands."

"And talked to him. Later he told me he could hear me sometimes. I know he could, too, because sometimes, when nobody else was around, I'd sing." Lannie smiled wistfully and flipped a hank of yellow hair behind her shoulder. "After he came to, he said I'd gotten the words wrong on one song."

"What song?"

"'Sweet Betsy From Pike.'"

Frankie grimaced. She would have picked a better song than *that*. "Don't sing that to Gorgeous. Pick something by Tammy Wynette."

"I don't have the nerve." She set George's feet down as though she were arranging them on a shelf, then covered them with the loose bed sheet. "We're never alone. He has such a large family."

"I hope we're not getting in your way," Frankie said stiffly.

"Oh, no, I didn't mean it that way. I know I..." Lannie backed into a chair and lowered herself slowly, as though she expected to be ordered to change her course any minute. "I don't really have any right or any claim."

"Yes, you do," Frankie admitted before she could bite the acknowledgment back. But she felt better for having said it. She stood and moved closer to the bed, trying to think of some way she might help George. She wasn't the foot-rubbing type.

The thin green line on the heart monitor rose and fell steadily. She should have been pleased with that much, but it was just up, down, up, down. She wanted *George* up. Up and awake and joking around.

She touched a fold in the sleeve of his hospital shirt. "What was it like when your brother finally woke up?" she asked Lannie.

"I wasn't there. I guess he asked for a pepperoni pizza."

"George is going to be hungry, too. That tube couldn't keep a bird fed." Frankie sighed, long and hard. "I can't stand seeing him like this."

She leaned down, close to his bruised face. "I hope you can hear me, Gorgeous. I hope you're in there listening. I'm getting tired of watching you just...just breathe and soak up this sugar water, and I want you to wake up and eat some frybread and—" She jerked her chin in Lannie's direction. "And to laugh at this woman and tell her to just leave your feet alone."

Lannie's eyes widened. Frankie planted her hands on her slim hips as she stood straight again. "I guess I'm not very good at this."

"You've known him longer than I have, Frankie, and if he recognizes anybody's voice, it'll probably be yours."

Maybe, Frankie thought. But then, she wasn't saying the right things. Impulsively she bent over the bed, braced her hands above her knees and got tough.

"If you don't wake up, I'm going to sing to you, right next to your ear. If you don't wake up, you'll have to listen. You can't stop me, Gorgeous. If Lannie did it to her brother, I can sure do it to mine." She glanced at Lannie, who was smiling. "Did Trey like your singing?"

"He didn't say."

"George says I sing like a crow."

Frankie hadn't noticed Luke standing in the doorway. "Is he talking about a Crow Indian, or a crow bird?" he wondered, and he laughed when Frankie jerked her head around. Her braid swung around and whacked her in the cheek.

"I don't know," she said as she tossed her hair back and tried to ease past her startled reaction. "Which is it, Gorgeous?"

"Doesn't matter," Luke answered for his brother. "Neither one can sing worth a damn."

Frankie stepped aside to let Luke take her place at George's bedside. He was dressed in crisp military khaki and ready to travel. Luke touched George's too-still shoulder, then sat on the bed beside him. "I've gotta be going now, Gorgeous, or they'll be sending out the MPs. You, uh…" He cleared his throat. "You want to wake up and tell me goodbye?"

This should have been a private moment between them, but Luke seemed to forget that the women were there, and Frankie's heart was suddenly too full, too heavy. She was unable to move away.

"Listen, brother, you've got a real bad habit of keeping people waiting." Luke took his brother's limp hand in his own. Amazingly, his voice was strong and steady. "Shake my hand, George. Before I go, just a small squeeze so I know…" He patted George's hand, then laid it on his stomach. "Okay. Be that way, then. Take your sweet time about it."

Lannie slipped from the room. Frankie heard her sniffle, and she couldn't blame her for it. Her own throat had burned shut. But when Luke started toward the door, she found enough voice to call his name. He waited a moment before he turned around, and she knew he was digging down for composure. She could share what she'd been hanging on to. Part anger. Part defiance. Part frustration. All good covers for fear.

"I want to find out who did this," she told him. "I want to know why."

"Chuck Two Hawk—"

"Chuck won't keep after it. If George doesn't tell us—"

"He will." He turned, spared a glance at the bed, then assured her, "I think so, Frankie. Very soon."

"But if he can't, then we'll never know what happened. They'll just say it was another drunk beaten up in another fight. Even if he wasn't drinking, they'll be saying he was, and pretty soon they'll have more important things to—"

He put his arms around her and gave her a hug. It was something he didn't do often, nor would she often succumb. Teasing was more their style. It didn't take much of a squeeze to tell her both take heart and goodbye. Luke cleared his throat again, and Frankie blinked furiously.

"Talk to Trey," he instructed. "He said he'd help."

"He's only interested in protecting his—"

"We don't know that."

"They haven't charged anybody, and they're never going to charge Race Latimer."

"I want you to talk to Trey." She started to turn away, but he grabbed her shoulder. "No, listen. Did you know that I once told Trey to stay away from you? Just like Race told George, only…" Frankie wanted to protest that one, but Luke raised that warning finger of his. "I had more reason," he told her. "You were fourteen going on twenty-one. He was my age, running on hormones, just like I was. My best buddy. I knew exactly what he was thinking whenever he looked at a girl. Hell, I was thinking the same damn thing. So I told him, not with my sister, you don't."

"Oh, for—"

"You had a bad crush on him then, Frankie. I knew it, and Trey damn sure knew it, too."

"Get—" she gave him a shove "—out of here."

He didn't budge an inch, of course.

"You should have seen your face every time I mentioned his name." Smiling now, Luke tugged at her braid. "It still gets a little funny."

"Quit that."

"I guess that's your normal face, huh? Funny looking?"

She scowled. The room was quiet, but they could hear Lannie talking to Hope out in the hallway.

"I feel like I'm running out on you, Frankie, but I've got no choice. My time is up."

"I know."

"I think you're right. Chuck Two Hawk doesn't have clue one right now about what happened to George. I don't think he's ruled Race out completely, and maybe I haven't, either."

"Daddy says it doesn't matter."

"You know Dad. He's been living on the rez too long."

She turned her head to look at George. To remind herself. "I think it matters."

"I want you to talk to Trey. He's not about to let this thing slide, no matter how temporary his job as sheriff is."

"He believes his brother."

"Which is exactly why he wants more answers. He wants everyone else to believe Race, too."

That made sense, in a way. She tried to think of who everyone else might be. Lannie, maybe? That woman sure was caught between the bull and the fence right now.

Frankie looked up at Luke. "What do you believe?"

"What I believe is that Gorgeous George is going to come to. And when he does, you and his skinny little woman are going to have to sit on him to hold him down."

"You really believe that." He nodded. Her oldest brother, who had seen the world. "Okay. I'll believe it, too. But just in case it isn't going to happen right away tomorrow, I'll talk to your friend."

"I'll be calling home. The fastest way for you to get hold of me is through the Red Cross." He tugged at her braid again before he gave her shoulder a quick squeeze. "You hang in there."

Frankie had to swallow some pride before she could keep her promise and make the drive out to the little place Trey had recently taken over. But Luke and Hope had left, and George seemed to be content to just lie there and let that skinny blond woman rub his feet forever. Frankie just couldn't hack it. If she couldn't make George wake up, she had to make something happen somehow. She decided to shake that towering-over-the-prairie Latimer tree up a little.

Nestled in the shadow of Rattlesnake Butte, the highest point in the area, the buildings of the old Bowker place weren't even visible from the gravel road. Frankie recognized the approach to the place and noted the name change on the roadside mailbox. She drove over two bumpy cattle guards before she could see that Trey's pickup was parked in front of his new house. As she drew closer, she could see that he was, too. Following the shade around the little white house on a hot Sunday afternoon was sure nice work, if you could get it.

From where Frankie sat she had a good view of the soles of his boots, propped up on a sawhorse. She knew he'd heard the car long before he finally lowered the front legs of his chair to the ground and eased the backrest away from the house's lap siding. He wasn't country anymore, she decided as she slowed to avoid a big, yellow dog that was howling at her left front tire. If he'd still been country, he would have picked up on the sound of a car slowing down at his place, and the coffee would have been brewing by now. But it looked as though Trey Latimer was hard-pressed to drag himself out of his chair. Probably didn't care if anybody ever came around for a second visit.

She parked her car in the newly graveled driveway, and they converged underneath a tall cottonwood in the front yard. He was bare-chested, and she wondered how he'd managed to tan that light skin so nicely if he spent his afternoons moving from one patch of shade to another. She jumped aside when something cold smeared something wet in the palm of her hand.

"Zeppelin, cut it out," Trey ordered, and the yellow dog waggled his apologies to his master.

"Zeppelin?"

"You ready for this?" He scratched the dog's head, ruffling his fur, and she could have sworn the animal was smiling at her, like *See, this is how you get his attention. Great, huh?*

No, she was not ready for this.

"I named him Zeppelin because, when I found him roaming around out here, he was full of buckshot. He must have tried to raid somebody's chicken coop or something." He looked up, his eyes smiling a whole lot prettier than the dog's. "And I had to get the lead out." He smiled at her, waiting. She glanced at the dog, then back to the smiling blue eyes. "Lead," he repeated, "Led Zeppelin?"

"That…is…sick." But she couldn't help smiling.

"Sick but true." He gave the dog one more vigorous scratching before giving him the order to lie down. Zeppelin picked a shady spot by the house.

"How's it going?" he asked. His tone had turned serious.

What was he expecting? Bad news, maybe. His gray eyes seemed guarded, but he did sound concerned enough to want an answer.

She wasn't going to give him an easy one. "That's what I came to ask you."

"You mean about suspects? You'll have to ask Two Hawk."

She didn't like his comeback, but she did like the broad cut of his shoulders. She always had. She didn't mind seeing him bared to the waistline of his beltless blue jeans.

He shifted his weight from one foot to the other. "Any change?" he asked finally.

"You mean about George?" she echoed. Then she reminded herself she hadn't come to spar with him. She shook her head to clear the sarcasm from her brain and sighed. "It's been two weeks now. Nothing."

He dragged his toe in the dust and kicked at a rock. She watched, wondering if that were to be the sum total of their conversation. He'd told her about his dog, and she'd told him about her brother. Luke had said, talk to Trey. So here they were. Talking.

"You want to come inside? I have cold pop, cold beer and cold water." He gestured toward the small white house. "Cold meat sandwiches, if you're hungry."

"How about air conditioning?"

"Sorry. Can't help you there."

On the way to the front door he took a quick detour to pick up some leather tack he had dropped on the ground next to the folding chair. He hopped up to the top of the stoop from the side, bypassing the steps, and opened the door for her. The gesture was startling. Frankie was accustomed to opening her own doors.

The house hadn't changed much since the early fifties, when it was built by a non-Indian couple who'd bought up some cheap Indian land. Nor had it changed hands until Trey bought the Bowkers out. Frankie wondered what changes he might make. There was nothing growing in the redbrick planter next to the steps, but the siding was newly painted. She'd only seen the house a few times from the top of the butte. She remembered it being painted sort of slime green.

She expected some kind of warning that the place was a mess, but none came. She was in for another surprise. Not all males were as messy as her brothers.

"This is neat," she said.

"It's pretty small." He looked around, as though refreshing his memory. "You're looking at practically the whole house. It has two bedrooms in the back."

The front was a living room and eat-in kitchen. Not much space was wasted on the hallway, where the door to the bathroom stood ajar.

"Have a seat," he said, but he claimed the easy chair by dropping his armload of tack on the floor next to it.

The yellow tank top she was wearing wasn't enough to keep her from sticking to the tan vinyl sofa, but she had to admit that it was nice vinyl—the pliant kind that could almost pass for leather. The few pieces of furniture and the braided rug on the hardwood floor all looked new.

She heard him open the refrigerator door.

"One more choice," he announced. "I've got iced tea."

"That would be good."

He returned carrying two glasses and wearing a plaid western shirt, which he hadn't snapped. The ice rattled in the glass he offered her. She straightened in the chair, and her skin peeled away from the vinyl like duct tape off a roll.

"That upholstery was a mistake," he said. "I bought it last spring, when the weather was a lot cooler."

"It'll be easy to keep clean."

It seemed a dumb thing to say, since it was probably the last characteristic she considered when she bought anything. He sat across from her in the easy chair, then hooked the toe of his boot under a matching hassock and dragged it closer, so he could go back to the comfortable boots-up position.

"Anyway, it all matches," she said.

"Is that good, or does it show my lack of imagination?"

"It's okay." She sipped her tea, impressed by the fact that it was brewed, not instant, and that he'd sweetened it and added just the right amount of lemon. "You could use a little more color in here."

"That's where I get into trouble. I'm color blind."

"Really?" Another flaw. That made two that she knew of, counting his scar, which was two more than she'd once thought he had. His relations probably wouldn't count as flaws. "You know, I've got nothing against you personally, Trey, even though—"

"What a relief," he said, and he shook his head, chuckling. "I knew I was on shaky ground anyway, but color blindness is always the killer."

"I'm talking about this thing with your brother and the way they let him go. But what I mean to say is, I guess I can't blame you for that."

"That *is* a relief." When she shrugged, he added, "Anyway, I haven't found any evidence that contradicts Race's story."

"Have you looked?"

"I've followed all the leads I know anything about. Beecher and Zahn, along with a few more people who were around town that night. The police found George's pickup in the same spot where Lannie last saw it. Nobody saw a fight. You know how fast a fight draws a crowd."

"Nobody saw him get in with anyone else?"

"Not so far."

"It wasn't a fight." She remembered telling him that before, and he'd pretty much agreed. "If it was, it was all one-sided."

"You're right about that. There were no bruises on George's hands." She lowered her glass from her lips in surprise, and he added, "I happened to notice."

"And he was clubbed on the head with something harder than a man's hand." Trey nodded in agreement. She figured she was doing pretty well so far, so she offered more. "George was rolled once, but he was dead drunk that time. I can't see anybody going after him for money when he was sober. And he *was* sober."

"Does he have any enemies?" He lifted his glass partway to his mouth, then glanced over the rim. "Other than my brother."

"Nobody as obnoxious as your brother." He didn't bite, but she protested anyway. "Lannie said it, if you remember."

"He has his good points. He's fair." He took a long drink, then reached down to set his tea on the floor. "I mean, if he's gonna go after somebody, it'll damn sure be somebody who can put up a good fight. Otherwise, he wouldn't be proving anything." Reaching down on the other side, he retrieved a partially braided rein from the pile he'd carried inside. "And Race has always had a bad need to prove himself."

"To who?"

"To Race."

He studied the worn strip of leather, which he'd apparently been reworking when she'd interrupted his afternoon. She wondered where he'd gotten the used tack and why he hadn't bought new stuff, like the furniture.

"You know what's funny?" There was no hint of humor in his eyes. "Race doesn't think I believe him. You think I do. I'm not doing too well either way. You both keep giving me that same look, like I just gave you a swift kick in the shin."

He was being dramatic. *She* certainly wasn't giving him any look. Squaring her shoulders, she explained carefully. "Somebody tried to kill George. I want to know who it was, and Luke thinks you can help me find out."

He straightened the three strands of leather and began braiding. "The real question is, why? Why would somebody try to kill George?" Sparing her a glance, he allowed, "You and I have come to some of the same conclusions, Frankie. It wasn't a fight or a simple assault that got out of hand. Somebody wanted George dead. You'd make a good cop."

The compliment brought the same rush of pleasure she'd known years ago, when they'd teamed up against George and Luke under the backyard basketball hoop, and Trey had whispered, "We're gonna be hard to beat, Frankie." The twinkle in those blue eyes was a photographic memory, but damned if she could remember who had won that time.

She smiled. "You told me that you were a good cop."

"But I'm not a cop anymore, good or otherwise. I'm just a temporary sheriff."

"I don't think so. I think you've done a lot of thinking and maybe a little snooping around that you don't want to admit to." She could tell she'd hit the nail on the head. "But I can't think of anybody besides your pig-headed brother who would want to hurt George."

"Race doesn't want to see him dead, Frankie."

"Then who does?" she asked in earnest.

"Somehow George must have gotten himself in somebody's way."

It was a good premise, but in the way to what? "Does your sister have another boyfriend?" she asked.

His response was a mirthless chuckle. "My sister is…I think you've used the word *nice*. Actually, she's good. She's the kind of woman men probably *should* fight over, but they don't." It seemed to sadden him, but he pushed that away with an impatient gesture. "No one's ever said to me, 'Trey, I would kill for a date with that sister of yours.'"

"And I've never heard anyone say, 'I'm going to kill George Tracker if he gets in my way.'"

He set the leather work aside and leaned forward, lacing his fingers together and considering her more intently. "We're missing some pieces, aren't we? Some pieces of George. Some pieces of Lannie."

"And maybe some pieces of Race?"

He tipped his head and briefly turned the corners of his mouth down. "Maybe."

"Wouldn't you like to know for sure? Then Race wouldn't have to prove anything."

"Right now it's Indian police business."

"You're the sheriff," she insisted.

"You know," he began as he picked up his glass and rose from the overstuffed chair, "I find it interesting that you want me in on this when I'd be up to my eyeballs in conflict of interest."

"Not if Race is innocent." Frankie followed him into the kitchen, taking her unfinished tea with her and countering his argument without missing a beat. "People around here are immune to this kind of thing. It happens all the time. Nobody does anything. What can you do? Indians get drunk, they beat each other up, and that's just the way it is," she recited.

Trey set his glass next to the sink, and Frankie followed suit. She didn't know whether he was listening anymore, but she wasn't finished. When he moved to the small window at the end of the room, she followed him there, too. He would hear her out.

"George was doing a lot better lately, since he started going with your sister. He was trying to make something of himself. It's not easy to make changes, you know. But he was giving it a real good shot."

He was about to push the ruffled white café curtain to one side, but she laid her hand on the crook of his elbow, arresting the motion, gaining his attention. She looked into his eyes deeply to make her impression. "I'm not going to just let it go."

For a long moment neither of them moved. His sleeve had been folded back, and her fingertips lay against his skin. Her palm collected the heat from the tenderest part of his arm. His gray eyes were like windows, unable to protect his emotions from her view. Her only challenge was to interpret them.

It was he who finally glanced away.

"I told you I was a good cop once. I wasn't satisfied with 'good cop.' I thought I had to be Super Cop, like in the movies." His wistful smile did not appear to be for her, but for something he saw outside the kitchen window. "You know, those guys in the movies use stuntmen. Makes a difference."

"The victims in the movies use ketchup. That makes a difference, too." She withdrew her hand from his arm, and it was as though the small room breathed a sigh around them. Whether of regret or relief, she didn't know. "I know it's been a long time since you and Luke were best buddies, but he still seems to think you hung the moon."

"Aw, jeez." His laugh was a little unsteady, but the tension dissipated, and he was able to tease. "That's hitting below the belt, Frankie."

"I hit a nerve?" She smiled, not totally unaware of

the coy flash in her eyes. "A soft spot, maybe? I'll have to remember that."

"It's a bad sign when a woman starts taking inventory of a man's soft spots."

"You probably don't have too many." She turned to the window. "You have quite a few horses?"

"I bought some quarter horses."

They both relaxed with the change of subject.

"I like that mare with the flaxen mane and tail," she said with real enthusiasm.

"Want to take a closer look?"

He led her outside. She watched his open shirt flap in the breeze as he headed for the newly refurbished corral. The rails had been treated to keep the horses from cribbing. Next to the barn lay a pile of discarded rails that bore evidence of destructive equine teeth. The barn had been given a fresh coat of red paint. He'd done a lot of work in a few short months.

"I didn't know you were a horse lover," she said as she peered between rails and picked out her favorite again.

The mare was built like a classic quarter horse, the mount for whom a fast quarter mile would be as easy to accomplish as a full day of working cattle. The contrast between the mare's chestnut body and her flaxen mane and tail gave her wonderful flash.

Trey rested one foot on the bottom rail and one hand on the top one. He squinted into the sun as he watched Frankie do the same. She wasn't copying him, she told herself, and she stood pat. It had been years since she'd been a follower of her brother's too-handsome friend.

The wind lifted his sun-gold hair, and he grinned at her. "Don't you remember how I used to hang around

your place hoping your dad would send Luke and me
out to run the cows in or fix fence? Any excuse to ride."

"I didn't notice. What I remember is the backyard basketball games at our place. You and Luke and George."

"We let you play sometimes." They looked at each
other, and he recalled, "Whenever I'd made the most points
in the last school game, I got to have you on my side."

"I don't remember anyone saying, 'I get Frankie on my
side.' It was more like, 'I get Gorgeous. You take Frankie.'"

And the boys had joked about skins and shirts, of
course, because Luke and George were "skins"—even
though they bristled to hear a white man use the term—
and they said Trey needed his shirt for protection. But
the boys were boys, and the three of them ran their
eyebrows up and down and elbowed each other about
keeping Frankie on the "shirt" side.

She had put up with it *most* of the time. It was the price
of having her presence permitted within inches of every
wonderful move her heroes made. At school she would
speak of these times as everyday occurrences and be the
envy of all her fellow underclassmen. She would even
repeat the "skins and shirts" jokes and talk about taking a
free swat at any one of them. Oh, that was some privilege.

She wondered if he remembered "skins and shirts"
when he caught her looking at his hair-peppered chest.
What she remembered was Trey's contrast with her
smooth-skinned brothers. His cocky grin banished the
years that had passed as he rubbed the heel of his hand
over his breastbone with slow deliberation.

"Does it itch, being hairy like that?" she asked.

"Sometimes, when I get in a sweat." He paused. She
watched his fingertips tangle with the curling hair. He
cleared his throat. "Like now."

"Most Indian men don't have hairy chests. Full-bloods don't." She glanced up at his face. "Is it prickly?"

He took her hand and pressed it over the part of him that held her fascination. His chest was warm, and she felt the drumbeat going on inside. His was harder, but hers was quicker. The smattering of hair tickled her palm, and the moisture she'd trapped there was a mingling from both of them.

"Is it?" he asked.

"No, I guess it isn't." She drew back slowly—her hand, then her gaze. The tickling lingered in her palm. She tried to shake it off with a quick flick of her braid and a light quip. "You've got a nice chest on you, Latimer. Like that mare." She glanced over the rail. "She's really built."

He laughed. "Built to please."

Yes indeed.

"We could go for a ride if you'd like," he offered.

Frankie turned away from the corral. "Maybe some other time." It was her turn to lead. His turn to follow. "What time does Lannie get off work?" she asked as she headed for the front yard.

"About 3:30. Why?"

"I told her I'd help her with her moving so she could get back up to the hospital and rub George's feet."

"She does that?"

She turned to get a look at the expression on his face, which matched the wonder in his voice. She found it so different from the way he'd been looking at her a moment ago that she had to stop and laugh. "It's really embarrassing sometimes," she said. "Lannie lovin' up George's little ol' pointy feet."

"I'll bet."

They stood beneath the cottonwood now. Trey's smile was soft, but it animated his eyes, and she couldn't imagine him lying in a hospital bed, pale and slack-jawed the way her brother was. He'd said he had. She suddenly realized she wanted his secrets, starting with a bad one. "What's it like to be unconscious?"

His smile faded. She could see him weighing the fragile trust that was growing between them. The leaves rattled softly overhead, warning them both of the risk of saying too much to someone who stood on the far side of any fence.

"It's like being alone in a tunnel." His voice was a match for the distance the memory placed between them. "Sometimes you see headlights way down at the end. But they go away."

He looked at her, and it was as though he'd gone somewhere and come back. His tone shifted, becoming instructive. "You don't know what's real and what isn't. One doctor told me that most of what I remember must be from just before I woke up, but I don't know. It felt like one long, bad dream."

In dreams she, too, had known bad times. She knew the fog and the fear, but she had no explanation for those things. Nothing as solid as the bullet that had hit his head.

"Do you hear people talking to you when you're unconscious?" she asked.

"It's not really a regular thing," he told her. "I mean, I try not to be unconscious too often." He was smiling again, and she knew her boldness in asking had been excused. Perhaps accepted.

He spoke freely now. "They said I responded some-times, or at least they thought I did. It's kind of like the morning after a party, when you have to ask people what you did when you were totally out of it. I knew something had been going on. There were voices with the headlights sometimes."

"Did you recognize…like, your wife's voice?"

"I recognized my little girl's." He thought a moment, and then he chuckled. "I know Lannie sang to me."

"No shame, that woman." She let the lighter thoughts drift away before she probed again. "Did you feel any pain?"

"I don't know, Frankie. It was like being in limbo." He shook his head, unable to define the term except to say, "With my head split open the way it was, limbo was probably a good place to be for a while."

"You were lucky, the way it turned out."

"Yeah." He rubbed the scar. The outward, visible sign of the way it had turned out. She guessed that there were many secrets beneath that puckered mark.

"I was planning on giving Lannie a hand with her big move," he said. "She told you to come today?"

"She's packing today, and I…" She didn't want to sound too much like the good little helper. "I figure it's something I can do for George."

He touched her arm lightly. She looked up and saw sympathy in his eyes. His touch felt good, and her heart warred with her pride. She needed to show him what she was made of and what a waste of time it would be to pity her.

"If you were going to look for those missing pieces, where would you start?" she asked.

He shoved his hands into his pockets and exhaled slowly. "I'd start with George. I'd backtrack from the time you found him, and I'd find out what he'd been doing, who he'd been seeing—what he'd said, what he'd signed, what he'd collected and spent. If it was a premeditated murder attempt, you'd be looking for a motive."

"He's been with the family a lot, especially since Luke's been home. Of course, he's been with Lannie."

"What's with these answers? Did I ask a question?" She offered no response, because she was busy with the pieces. More pieces. "Frankie, Chuck Two Hawk is a very good—"

"He's been with one other person," she recalled.

"Oh, yeah? Who?"

She smiled. That was definitely a question. "A man he was supposed to be getting into some construction business with."

"New business or existing business? Had he been offered a job?"

"No, but I think they were planning to get something going. I don't know what, exactly." She did know that the questions were multiplying nicely. "George is always getting into something that doesn't work out for him, so when he tells me about a new plan, I usually just wait and see what happens."

"Do you know the man's name?"

"I'll bet Lannie would know. I think she's got some real heavy things that need packing." She smiled appreciatively. "Good workout for this nice chest of yours."

Chapter 5

Trey Latimer was hooked. He knew it. His brain was buzzing, and for a change it had nothing to do with pain or the attempt to alleviate it. It was the old excitement of finding a couple of scraps of information, curious little pieces he knew to be shards of something bigger. He was on his way to Mobridge, which was the place to start testing the angles to see where they might fit. He had a hunch that the something bigger was the construction business. He was going to find out.

Maybe Frankie was right about the need to obliterate any suspicion about Race. He told himself they were her suspicions—maybe Two Hawk's, possibly others'—but none of his own. The bits and pieces would add up to proving them wrong. But mostly they would add up to answers. And he liked being the one to find the answers.

He was probably hooked in more ways than one. Clever angling on Frankie's part, he thought. He knew damn well he'd enjoyed every minute of playing into her hands. Her fingers had felt just fine against his skin in the heat of the day. Not that she'd been climbing all over him or anything, but it seemed as though he'd tuned in to a new variation on everybody's favorite old theme, the mutual attraction of male and female.

Later, when they had gone to help Lannie, the hook had lodged itself even deeper. More interesting bits, more fascinating pieces. Lannie had supplied the name of George's prospective partner, Craig Pratt, who was trying to expand his carpentry business. George had some construction experience, but he had something more important to offer. He was an enrolled Indian. Pratt was anxious to bid on federally funded reservation jobs, and Trey figured that a non-Indian carpentry business would have a better chance of getting the nod if there were an Indian partner.

Lannie had confirmed his theory. For the better part of what had been left of that day, she'd had him taking her glass shelves apart while she and Frankie wrapped her endless collection of porcelain dolls in a mountain of tissue paper. He hadn't minded. It was about time Lannie got out of that house, and he was about the only one supporting the move, besides Frankie.

Frankie hadn't paid much attention to the details of George's business plans, but she knew a little about Indian preference with the B.I.A. Between the two women and over a Phillips screwdriver, he had gathered that George had been looking for a steady job, and Pratt had been pretty open about the advantages George could bring to his business.

Trey remembered feeling like a bull in a china closet, but it was the good feeling of helping the sister he'd nearly lost touch with that had made his day. That, and watching Frankie wrap those prissy dolls....

"So, what does George think of all this?" Trey asked as he dropped another screw into the metal toolbox.

Lannie spoke defensively. "He thinks it's a start. And he also thinks it's right. It's a good chance for an Indian to actually get into a business that's operating on the reservation."

"He'd be fronting for this Pratt, wouldn't he?"

"To start out with, maybe. But George is smart, and he's a good worker."

"He's had construction jobs," Frankie added. "Lots of them."

Suddenly it was two on one, and Trey realized that Lannie had sounded almost as spunky as Frankie did, which pleased him. Gorgeous George was quite an inspiration.

"All he's lacking is venture capital."

"Says my sister the banker," Trey teased. "What are we going to do with all this glass when I get these brackets apart?"

"See that newspaper over there?" She pointed to a stack that would have kept a litter of puppies doing business for a long time. "We're going to use that for the shelves. And my dishes. You know, I have my own dishes."

Trey surveyed the bedroom that had long been "Off Limits" to him and Race. He remembered sneaking in to snatch a piece of the Christmas candy she'd always hoarded and never eaten. Finding it was always the challenge.

"My God, you've got a lot of stuff, Lannie. Don't you ever throw anything away?"

"Not very often," she admitted happily. Frankie handed her another tissue-wrapped doll, and she laid it carefully in what looked like a box of little mummies. Trey wondered if Tricia was old enough for this kind of stuff yet.

"Dad won't get mad if I take Mother's cedar chest, will he?" Lannie asked. "She gave it to me."

"Then it's yours. And anything else that came from her side of the family." He surveyed the room again. "Like this bed."

"Ohh, Grandmother's spool bed." It had been Lannie's bed as long as either of them could remember, but she was hesitant. "Do you really think I should?"

"Do you have a place to put it yet? I'll load it up for you."

"I don't know," Frankie said, assessing the old bed. She was dressed, as usual, in faded jeans and a summer top. Never any frills for Frankie. Trey wondered what she thought of Lannie's pink eyelet coverlet and the pile of little pink-and-white pillows. The pink looked grey to him, because he had trouble with all but the darkest shades of red and green, but pink had always been Lannie's choice, just as it was always pink for Tricia. He tried to imagine Frankie's bed.

But his imaginings were cut short when she sat right down in the middle of all the eyelet, put the soles of her bare feet together and pulled them up to her seat so that she could lean over her knees and peer down. She didn't need ruffles, Trey thought, even though she looked fine in the midst of them. She was all lithe and lovely woman.

"It's pretty high off the floor. Gorgeous has been

known to fall out of bed. Not only that, but…" Frankie straightened, then swiveled from her waist, taking in the foot of the bed, then the head. "I don't think it's big enough." Her eyes danced when she looked up at Lannie and jerked her thumb over her shoulder toward the west wall. "I think you ought to take the one in that room, as long as Trey's doing the loading up."

"That's Dad's bed. Oh, wouldn't he just be livid?" Lannie enjoyed the prospect, but she decided against it. "I'd rather have Grandmother's bed. It'll be cozier. We'll have to really cuddle up."

"You two are making me blush," Trey said.

Even now, as he finished off a cigarette and rode the waves of the buckling highway that led to Mobridge, he had a hard time thinking of Lannie sleeping in that antique bed with a man. *Any* man. And it wasn't because she wasn't attractive enough or that she hadn't waited long enough. It was because she was his sister.

On the other hand, he was having a hard time *not* thinking about the way Frankie had looked sitting cross-legged in the middle of that puffy pink comforter on Lannie's bed. He thought of the way she had tossed her long, silky black hair behind her shoulder when she'd caught him admiring her, the way she'd parted her lips, just slightly, and stared back at him. He wanted to unbind that hair sometime, comb his fingers through it and see whether it reached the back pockets of her jeans.

He crossed the big bridge and took the turn he had been conditioned to dread. His investigation had brought him round to his father's front door. The door to his precious business this time. The redbrick building on the outskirts of Mobridge housed the offices of L & M

Construction, formerly Latimer Construction. If the construction industry held the answers Trey was seeking, it made sense to start at the top.

This was the first time Trey had actually noticed the name of the new partnership, which was not the alliance Phillip Latimer had once envisioned. But a father and son partnership, at least the one Phillip had wanted, would have been a disaster. Trey might have been spared a shattered head, but his sanity would have snapped long ago. He and the old man had been bad news together since he was about twelve years old.

The receptionist directed Trey to his father's newly decorated office. Potted plants and posters of city skylines were a nice touch in the reception area, but totally out of keeping with the man who maintained strict control by compartmentalizing everything in his life. He had comfort at home, function on the job, and his fun out of town only.

"Things sure look different around here," Trey said as he took the chair he was offered. "Business must be good."

His father looked better than he had the last time Trey had seen him. He was relaxed, for one thing. "Business has always been good. Messner likes the up-holstered chairs and the artwork on the walls."

"You've been working hard all your life. You can afford to indulge yourself a little." Maybe even get yourself out of those tan coveralls and into some kind of shirtsleeves.

"I guess you could say that. God knows I've indulged everybody else." He eyed Trey pointedly. "You three do whatever you want with your lives. I oughta do the same."

"If you're talking about Lannie, Dad, she needs a place of her own. She's taken care of you and Race and the house—"

"Fine." Phillip dismissed the issue with the flick of a hand. A sore spot, Trey guessed. And no traffic signal was more decisive than that hand. "So, what finally brings you out here?"

"Checking out the construction business," Trey said, shifting uneasily in his chair. He didn't enjoy playing detective with his father. "How's your new partner working out?"

"He's brought in some business." Phillip fanned through a stack of folders on his desk. "He's out in Aberdeen right now working on some people."

"Working on *people?*"

"We've all got our talents."

"You never used to have much interest in politicking. What kind of people is he working on?"

"Government people, I guess." He pushed the folders aside. "Business is business. We're trying to expand in a slow economy, like everybody else. You know, diversify. We're looking at jobs in a five-state area now."

"The only government people in Aberdeen are B.I.A."

Phillip nodded. "That's right. Lots of federal contracts up for grabs."

Terrific.

It was his job to ask questions, but he had a feeling he didn't want any more answers.

"Don't Indian-owned companies still get preference on jobs like that?" Trey asked.

"If they look good enough to handle the job, they get the contract." Phillip leaned back and crossed his arms over his chest. "Most of those outfits fold up eventually for lack of capital. Usually there's no backing and not much experience. And when they can't deliver, we get the job."

"You could have cinched it." It was a suggestion

Trey had intended to avoid. "You could have made Race a partner."

"Race doesn't have a lick of business sense."

"And you didn't know he was enrolled."

Phillip glared for a moment, but the hand dismissed the issue once again. "Wouldn't have mattered. I don't believe in Indian preference, or affirmative action, or whatever the popular term is. Race has to compete in this world, just like the rest of us. All he wants to do is work his forty-hour week and raise hell on weekends."

"It seems only fair to give Indian businesses some kind of preference on the reservation."

"Yeah, well, it would." He leaned forward to jab the air with an accusing finger. "To you. You've always been a bleeding heart."

They exchanged heated stares, but Trey held his peace.

Phillip glanced away. "I've never had anything against those people, but business is business. You want the job done right, you come to a reputable company like Latimer Construction."

"L & M Construction," Trey corrected. By the look in his father's eyes, he figured the new name must have been yet another sore spot. The damn sore spots were mounting up fast. Time to get to the point. "What do you know about Craig Pratt's outfit?"

"It's not much of an outfit. It's one man with a couple of apprentices. Pretty good finish carpenter, though, from what I hear."

"No competition for you?" Phillip shook his head. "Had you heard anything about a partnership between Pratt and George Tracker?" Trey asked.

Phillip chortled. "Partners in what? Keeping the bars in business?"

"George has some experience."

"There's a big difference between working construction and running a—" Phillip's fist came down on the desk. "There, you see? Perfect example."

"Of what?"

"Working the damn system. The whole damn country's on the dole," he expounded as he shoved his chair back and got to his feet. "Well, you won't catch me doing it. You ought to be able to put in an honest bid and expect to be considered strictly on the merits of that bid and what stands behind it. Business is by damn *business*."

"Business is definitely business."

As usual, Phillip had no idea what Trey was talking about. Irony was lost on him.

"I told you it was crazy to get into the horse business. It's not a business. It's a hobby. You're going to find yourself throwing good money after bad, and you're going to wonder what in hell you were thinking when you—"

"I've wondered about some of the things I've done. But not the horses," Trey said, fully realizing that his father had no interest in his thinking. Still, he explained, "I like them. I like feeding them and watching them run."

"Two great reasons for sinking your savings into—"

"I enjoy riding them. I don't even mind shoveling up their manure." He smiled as he rose from the chair. "Horse manure stinks, but it makes things grow. So it's good for something. Thanks for your time, Dad."

Over the course of the next two days, Trey's temporary job promised to become a semipermanent pain. He was called in on a neighbors' squabble, a break-in and a trespassing complaint. They all turned out to be the nuisance kind of stuff he hadn't missed at all. But he made a point of paying a visit to Craig Pratt, just to do a little more fishing. All he got for his effort was impressions, but even that made it worth driving up to Fort Yates to compare notes with Two Hawk.

Big Chuck had a little cubicle at the Indian police station. It was tight quarters for a man his size, but it was an office of his own, and he was hospitable. He offered Trey coffee and the use of an ashtray. Trey figured there was enough smoke in the air already. He asked Two Hawk what he'd turned up on the Tracker case, and when the policeman sighed and shook his head, Trey told him about George's business plans.

Two Hawk listened with interest before adding his thoughts. "The B.I.A. is wising up. You can't just hire an Indian off the street to get him to call you blood brother. Is Pratt looking for Indian preference, just flat out?"

"I asked him what kind of jobs they might be looking at, but he was pretty vague. He said they were still working on incorporation." He replayed the meeting in his head, recalling the tone of Pratt's voice and the steady eye contact. "He seemed concerned about George. Apparently George has done a lot of work for him in the past, and he thought maybe they had something to offer each other."

"You know who's got all those jobs sewn up around here right now, don't you?"

Trey picked up a black ballpoint pen and clicked the cartridge, then clicked again. He eyed Two Hawk. He knew damn well he was being tested. "You're gonna tell me it's my father."

"You got it," Two Hawk quipped with a bob of his head. "So it comes back to the Latimers again. You just can't win with this, can you?"

"Every construction company in the area bids on those contracts. My father's too old to run around beating up on all his competition."

Two Hawk leaned back, stretching the limits of the flexible desk chair, and laced his fingers together at the back of his neck. "So he sends your brother out to narrow it down some."

"Come off it, Chuck. This isn't New York or L.A." Trey tossed the pen back on the desk. "If he were willing to go to all that trouble, why didn't he just use Race to front for a by-Indian bid?"

"Or make Race a real partner."

"I'd like to see him do that, but not for the reasons—"

"The reason is money, and people do it for that reason all the time." Two Hawk retrieved the black pen and scribbled the name on a yellow pad. "What did you think of Pratt?"

"I got the feeling that he does a good, solid job and that he likes George. He said he hasn't decided what to do about their plans. He's 'on hold,' is what he said, hoping George recovers."

Two Hawk nodded slowly, considering the name on the pad for a moment before he glanced up. "Did you know they transferred George down here to the Indian hospital yesterday?"

"I hadn't heard."

The policeman shook his head. "Poor old George. I knew another guy, got himself—"

The dispatcher happened by, coffee mug in hand. "You talking about George Tracker?" he wondered innocently. "Carmine Bone Club called over from the clinic. Gorgeous George just woke up and kissed his sweetheart good morning."

Two Hawk was out of his chair and out the door almost as fast as Trey was.

At the mention of George Tracker, a nurse directed them down one of the small hospital's three short corridors. Lannie's beaming face was the bright light at the end of it. She was bursting beautifully with the news.

"The doctors are in there now. His eyesight seems a little shaky, but he saw me. He said my name." As exuberant as Trey had ever seen her, she welcomed him with a quick hug. "Oh, Trey, he knew who I was. He's going to be fine now. I kissed him, and he kissed me back."

"That should do it. Kissing is the best medicine."

"Kissing is good for people. It is definitely—" She pulled away and started down the hall. "Nobody was home at the Trackers when the nurse called before. I'm going to try again."

"We'll put out a police bulletin," Two Hawk told her.

But Trey wanted to have a particular Tracker there. "How about Frankie?"

"She wasn't at her apartment." Poised to take off down the hall, Lannie reminded Trey of a pebble in a slingshot.

"I'm gonna try her at school." He caught up to her, figuring there was a phone behind every desk. It had been a while since he'd been bursting at the seams this way.

"School's not open yet," Lannie told him as she claimed the first phone they found.

"She said she had things to do there." And he wanted to be the one to tell her. He found a pay phone in the lobby.

The janitor tracked her down at school while Trey waited on his end, grinning at the numbered buttons until she finally answered.

"Frankie? Trey. I'm up in Yates at the clinic, and I

was just wondering when you're coming by to say hello to your brother."

"This evening. After I get my classroom—" There was a pause. "What's going on?"

"A little miracle, I guess. I haven't talked to him yet, but Lannie has."

"Talked? He *talked?* When?"

"Just a little while ago. They've been trying to get in touch with your parents."

He tried to imagine the look on her face as she sputtered, "Oh, no, they took the younger kids…they all went…I'll be there *really* quick."

He got a kick out of the way she emphasized *really*. He could just imagine that little car turning into a blue bullet on the highway.

Two Hawk was head-to-head with a doctor outside George's room when Trey returned. He was surprised that Chuck introduced him into the conversation as "sheriff of Corson County and part of our team."

"I understand that George is back with us." Trey glanced past the doctor's white coat and caught a glimpse of a nurse and the back of Lannie's head, but he couldn't see George.

"He's regained consciousness, yes. He's confused, but he's aware."

"I'd like to talk to him if—"

"We don't want to burden him with too many questions right now. He's confused and really quite scared."

Two Hawk explained. "Dr. Reinhof is one of the specialists we get down here from Bismarck on a monthly basis. He's here for eye clinic today. Lucky thing it happened to be today."

The three of them took turns glancing into the room

as they spoke. Trey was anxious to catch the sound of George's voice, so long silenced, now free to give those answers he'd been looking for.

"There's not much I can do here," Dr. Reinhof said. "I don't have the equipment to run the kind of tests we need. It looks as though we have some damage to the right eye."

"No wonder he's scared," Two Hawk said.

"Well, he's a little fuzzy in other ways, too, but right now we're taking it as it comes."

Trey ventured into George's room, expecting to be kicked out anytime. Lannie was all smiles, but the leathery nurse who was keeping close tabs on George's vital signs eyed him suspiciously.

"Did the doctors clear you to come in here? We're allowing family only."

He charmed the older woman with a smile. "I'll be family soon if my sister has her way."

It was good to see Lannie's face so full of joy. And George. He was pallid and dazed, like a man who'd just emerged from a long stay in a deep cavern. His right eye was covered with gauze. But he was awake.

Trey moved to the foot of the bed. "Welcome back, Gorgeous."

With his eyelid at half-mast, George managed a wan smile. "Gorgeous George. Tha's m-me."

"Feels like you've been sleeping for a month, doesn't it?"

George's lips barely moved, and each word came laboriously. "Feels like…ah bin…dead."

"I know what you mean. I've been there myself."

George didn't seem to know or care who Trey was or where he'd been. Trey remembered that awful confusion in the beginning, that sense of being out of step with everything around you.

"Frankie's on her way up here. I just called her." Trey glanced at Lannie, then back at George, who was unimpressed with the news. "Frankie, your sister."

George groaned and flopped his hand at his side. "Can't see good."

"It'll take a while to get everything back, George."

"Head hurts."

"I know." Trey's palms were damp. He worked his way around the bed, moving closer to Lannie. He knew it hurt her, too. "It's bad at first, but it gets better."

He remembered it well. Right now, it didn't matter to George what had caused it. All that mattered was the fear of splitting apart. But the cause mattered to Trey, because it angered him, and because he had work to do. He might not get another chance like this.

Trey bent down close to George's ear. "Who was it, George? Who did this to you?"

"Somebunny mussa...hit me."

"Did you see who it was?"

"Mo-bige." The light dawned in one cloudy brown eye. "Where's Lannie?"

"I'm right here." She moved in and took his hand.

"You okay?" George asked wearily. "You got home okay?"

"I'm fine. I'm so glad to see you, George." She turned to Trey and pleaded softly, "Let him rest. He can't think about that now."

Disappointed, Trey backed off. Two Hawk was waiting to see how much Trey could get. Their eyes connected, and Trey shook his head. Damn little.

"The important thing is that he's turned the corner," Two Hawk said.

"That's right." He was happy for Lannie. George was a lucky man, to make it back and find love waiting for him. Trey turned to the nurse. He knew she wouldn't tell him much. "How are his reflexes?"

"Slow, but that's no surprise." She directed his attention to the two men who were about to enter the room. "You'll have to give the doctors some room now."

Two Hawk went back to the police station, but he asked Trey to keep him informed of anything else he learned, promising to reciprocate. It was an awkward situation on all fronts. Most crime victims looked on the police as the best hope for redress, but not on the reservation. Two Hawk was probably aware that Frankie had no faith in his police force. Trey hadn't earned her confidence; he'd gained it by default. The long-standing lack of respect for the Indian police was ingrained in her thinking.

They couldn't be trusted. They worked for the B.I.A., which stood for "Bossing Indians Around." They'd turned on their own people, starting with Sitting Bull, and more recently on Pine Ridge Reservation in '73, when activists and traditional Indians had clashed with the FBI and the Indian agencies empowered by the Federal Government.

Trey remembered. He understood the spot Two Hawk was in better than he understood his own role in all this. In his own mind, he had to be acting unofficially. Helping out where he could. If he could. As he ventured across the street for a pack of cigarettes, he turned the situation over in his mind, trying to come up with the best way to let Two Hawk know where he stood. Two Hawk's badge was permanent. His was just temporary.

He had himself a smoke on the back steps of the clinic's hospital wing. From there he could watch the river roll by, catching the sun's rays in its ripples. His head had started pounding, and he knew it was a mistake to finish the cigarette, but it tasted too good to put out. He braced his elbows on the low brick wall and let the breeze cool his face. He'd broken a sweat, and the air felt good.

Aspirin was all he carried for the pain these days. The fact that the pain put him in close touch with George somehow lifted the burden and put the situation into better perspective. The pain came first. The pain would always come first until you learned to move past it.

The blue hatchback skirted around the corner and into the hospital parking lot. Trey ditched the cigarette on his way down the steps. He wanted to open the big double doors for her and walk her down the hall. He wanted to see the look on her face when she saw the miracle.

She was excited. She couldn't walk or talk fast enough. "I've left messages everywhere for my parents. They're out buying school clothes." Trey stretched his steps to stay abreast of her and enjoy the animated expression in her eyes as she peppered him with questions. "How is he? Same old Gorgeous? Is he on his feet yet? Is he—"

"Be patient, Frankie. He'll need some time to heal. Surgery, maybe, I don't know. But the worst fear is past."

"That whole coma thing was the worst," she said. Her voice was strong and confident, now that it was safe to speak of the worst out loud. "Worse than death, I think."

He hadn't meant to give her the impression that everything was back to normal, but neither did he want to take away the initial joy. He would leave that to the man who was hanging out in the hallway with the ever-present chart in his hands.

"Dr. Reinhof, this is George's sister, Frankie."

She paused, but she only had eyes for the door to George's room.

"You want to see your brother first, then see me." Frankie nodded and started to move away, but the doctor wasn't finished. "You're going to ask me about his right eye, and I'm going to have to say I don't know yet. There's been some kind of damage. I can't say how much. Maybe we can repair it. Maybe it will repair itself. Maybe it isn't, uh…right now we just don't—"

Right now she wanted to see for herself. With another quick nod she left the doctor standing there with his hand still midgesture.

Trey excused himself and hurried after her. He claimed a position just inside the door, while Lannie backed away from the bedside to make room for Frankie.

"Well, Gorgeous, you old sleeping beauty, you finally woke up." She sat beside him on the bed, studying his face and giving him a chance to do the same. "Don't you know who I am?" George only stared. "Don't you know Frankie?"

"Frankie," he repeated.

"That's right." She touched his shoulder tentatively. "Your sister, Frankie."

"Where's Mom?"

"She's coming. They took Sweetie and Crystal out to buy clothes. School's starting pretty soon." Frankie sat up straight, pressed three fingers to her lips and looked for Trey. Her eyes glistened, and he tried to tell her, with a smile and a slight nod that all would be well. Her hand came down, and she nodded, too, then brightened as she turned back to George. "You slept away half the summer."

"Where's Luke?"

"He had to go, George. The army transferred him over to Germany, remember? He stayed as long as he could, and I'm supposed to call him." He was drifting. She touched his hand and offered an incentive to keep him awake. "You want to talk to him?"

"Can't see good." His chin inched toward his right shoulder. "Tired."

"Jeez, you've been sleeping for—"

But George closed his good eye, and Frankie wasn't going to talk him out of it. It scared her, and she cast around the room for help. "What's the matter? Is he going back—"

Lannie laid a hand on her shoulder. "He's tired. He dozes in and out. The doctor says it's okay."

Trey went to Frankie's side, and she let him usher her toward the door. When she looked back, he put his arm around her, and she turned to him with a faint plea in her eyes. Help her believe, he thought. Fairness exists outside the weather forecast.

"What kind of damage?" she asked. "Is it just the one eye, or is there more?"

"They don't know yet, Frankie. He's like a chick coming out of his shell. It's hard work. He's gotta take his time."

They stood together in the hallway. Frankie shook her head as a kitchen worker pushed a cart past them. "He didn't know me. I had to tell him who I was."

"He knew Lannie. That's a good—"

"A good sign? Why should he know her and not me?"

"What matters is that he knew somebody. Lannie's his…" He shrugged, unable to think of a more suitable term. "His girl. She loves him, and I think her love somehow penetrated the darkness for him."

"You think she brought him out of it?"

"Maybe she helped. He knows that something bad happened to him, and he asked her if she was okay." He squeezed her shoulder, hoping she would smile again. "Face it. He loves her, too."

Frankie chuckled. "Does it sound like I'm jealous?"

"Maybe a little."

"George has had a ton of girlfriends. He's Gorgeous George."

"Lannie's different."

"That's for sure." They looked at each other for a moment, counting the differences mentally until they both laughed. Frankie tipped her head back and grinned at the ceiling. "I don't care. They can be as lovey dovey as a sappy old movie for all I care. George is back among the living, and that's what counts."

Suddenly she clamped her hands around Trey's arm and gave it a quick shake. "I've gotta call Luke. Help me find a phone so I can call Luke."

"Try the nurses' station."

She put a call in through the Red Cross, and it wasn't long before Luke called back. Trey started to walk away, to mind his own business while she was on the phone, but she grabbed him by the arm and hauled him back. The move amazed him. Her smile stirred him, and he let her anchor him there until she'd told Luke the news. It surprised Trey when she handed him the phone.

"Go on. You can probably tell him more than I can." She pressed the phone, warm from her ear, against his. Her eyes sparkled, and she goaded him with a quick thrust of her chin. "Tell him about love piercing the darkness. Luke's in love, too. He'll probably like that all over."

Chuckling, Trey shouted across the miles of land and sea. "Hey, Luke, how come this sister of yours is such a smart aleck?"

"Are you chasing after my sister again, buddy?" teased the familiar voice that sounded too far away.

"No way. She's chasing after me. She thinks I'm some kind of private detective or something. Straight out of some—" She was hanging on to his shoulder, her eyes full of excitement again. He winked at her. *"—old movie."* Then, more seriously, "He's not out of the woods yet, Luke, but he looks good. He sounds good, considering what he's been through."

"Did he say anything about what happened?"

Trey exchanged a glance with Frankie. "He's just come out of a coma, and he doesn't know what hit him. That's natural."

"Sure. The main thing is that he's coming around." There was a pause. "You're gonna keep after it, aren't you, Trey?"

"I'll do my best."

"Can't ask for more than that."

That wasn't exactly true. Luke could have asked for a lot more than a broken-down ex-cop who'd been trying to put himself out to pasture with a quiet herd of quarter horses. He'd taken a bullet in his thigh once, and he'd been back in there swinging within a month. But a head injury was something else. It had put him off balance. It had made him as heady-shy as an abused horse. And it had destroyed his sleep.

He handed the phone back to Frankie and waited until she'd said goodbye. They looked at each other, remembering the teasing and the sound of Luke's voice and the way they'd shared the call. He took her hand from the receiver and held it, rubbing his thumb over her knuckles to reassure her.

"Listen, I'd better get out of the way here, but I want to talk to you a minute before I take off."

"You're not in the way." She looked at him quizzically. "Did you ask George anything about what happened yet?"

"I shouldn't have, but I did. He doesn't know."

"Doesn't know, or doesn't remember?"

"It's too early to ask him that." He drew her away from the nurses' station. No one was listening, but it seemed as good an excuse as any to keep his hold on her hand. He saw the expectancy in her eyes. "But I have talked to Craig Pratt."

"George's partner?"

"The incorporation papers haven't been processed, but George's *intended* partner, yes. How much can you tell me about these by-Indian contracts?"

"Indian businesses get preference on some federal jobs." She slid her hand from his. "It's only fair to give us the edge for once. After all, non-Indian businesses have made—"

"I know. I'm not questioning the principle. I'm just backtracking, looking for pieces. We know that's probably what they were going after, but I don't know exactly what kind of an agreement they were working on. Pratt was playing it pretty close to the chest." He shrugged as he shoved his hands into his pockets. "Probably because I'm Phillip Latimer's son, which adds a wrinkle for him, too." He hesitated, then gave her the rest. "My father's company also bids on those federal contracts."

"And George was threatening to give him some competition," she concluded.

"There's all kinds of competition," he said. "I need to find out who else might be in the running."

"Craig Pratt would probably know."

"He might. I need to visit him again. First time around, you just ask a few questions and try to get a feel for attitudes."

"Clever." They were moving down the corridor together now. She wasn't going with him, but she was thinking with him, which drew her along. "So, what's Pratt's attitude?"

"Cautious. Careful, at least around me. But he doesn't strike me as a user."

"You mean, you don't think he's using George?"

"That's one of those gray areas. He seemed concerned about George's health, but there could be lots of reasons for that. I don't know enough about it yet to figure in all the possible deviations." They'd reached the side exit. He braced his arm on the push bar and turned, arching an eyebrow. "So far, I'm just fishing."

"Well, I'm hunting. The next time around, I want to go with you to talk to Mr. Pratt."

"Don't you trust me?"

"Not if your father is George's main competition." He gave her a look of disgust. She shrugged. Then she smiled. "Not completely, anyway."

They visited Pratt the following day. It was pretty unorthodox for Trey to take Frankie along, but the whole thing was pretty unorthodox. He decided he would rather have her right next to his elbow, where he could be sure she wasn't "hunting" on her own.

She decided she wanted to watch him work. And she wanted to meet Craig Pratt, the man who was interested in finding himself an Indian for a business partner.

Pratt was a middle-aged, soft-spoken man who was quick to offer a handshake, but slow to put his work aside and have a talk. They waited while he finished routing a nice piece of oak molding. Then he offered them coffee and a seat on a bench next to the wall.

"So George is doing better," Pratt said as he seated himself on a tall wooden stool. "That's good news. Did you know that George has worked for me on a couple of sites? He's a damn good carpenter and, of course, now that he's straightened his life around…"

"But that's not why you want to make him a partner," Frankie said. She ignored the assertive glance Trey shot her. Why should he do all the talking?

"He came to me a few months ago looking for work, and I told him I couldn't use him unless I picked up more business. We got to talking about the Indian housing program, and we came up with this idea." Pratt glanced from Trey to Frankie, then back again. "It's not revolutionary, I know, but we're not trying to put anything over on anybody. I'm equipped for the jobs they're bidding out—the smaller ones, anyway. With George as a partner, we'd have a good chance of getting the bid."

"George's only experience is in labor," Frankie pointed out.

"Mine was, too. He'll learn. We figured on hiring Indian labor. If it went well here, we could bid on jobs down at Cheyenne River Reservation, too."

"Any competition besides L & M?" Trey asked.

"Not that I know of." Pratt spread his hands wide. "I'm really not looking at the competition. We're just putting in our bid. Somebody else might be putting something together, too."

"What if you don't get the bid?" Frankie asked. "Is George out?"

"If George hadn't gotten hurt, he was in, regardless. And we'd keep trying." He turned to Trey. "I've been thinking about this since the last time you were here. I did have a phone call about a month back. I didn't take it too seriously then. No name. Just a warning that I ought to stick with what I knew and stay away from the Indian contracts."

Frankie looked at Trey, too, but he betrayed no reaction to the news. Not so much as a blink, while Frankie could almost hear the voice of George's attacker in that threat. She squirmed in her seat close to him on the bench.

"Why didn't you call the police?" Trey asked as he put his hand on the wood between them. Frankie felt the pressure of his little finger against the outside seam of her jeans.

"There was no real threat attached," Pratt claimed. "Just 'you *ought to* stick to what you do best,' or something like that."

"Sure sounds like a threat," Trey said matter-of-factly. "Why didn't you tell me about it when I was in before?"

"You're a Latimer. I didn't know you were a friend of the Trackers."

Frankie made a supreme effort and held her tongue until they were inside Trey's pickup. She almost made it, but he had to go and open the door for her, which put him right there, ripe for the asking.

"What are you going to do?"

"I'm going to follow up on that phone call," he said quietly. "Get in."

"Follow it up how?" He ignored her. She climbed into the passenger seat and let him shut the door, but the minute he was behind the wheel, she blurted out, "What will you do if it leads to your brother? Or your father?"

"It doesn't matter where it leads. Officially or unofficially, I have to finish what I've started." He started the pickup before he turned to her, his gray eyes at once cool and intense. "Believe it or not, Frankie, I don't hold with looking the other way for anybody."

Chapter 6

Frankie had a way with sheets. In her classroom an old bed sheet could become a tent one day and a costume the next. She kept a good supply of them handy, along with cardboard boxes, plastic milk jugs and other imagination liberators. She had little more than a week to get organized. She knew the workings of the seven-year-old mind, and she knew that the pastel-striped tipi she'd built over the new classroom computer would beckon the curious.

Everything was set—the red ball of fuzz with eyes and feet sitting atop the monitor on a low shelf, and the pillow on the floor, where a child naturally wanted to sit. She flipped the power switch, called up the directory, then ducked outside to see whether she'd achieved the illusion of a fire glowing within the tent.

She nearly jumped out of her jeans.

Trey was sitting there on her desk, laughing at the way she clutched her shirt to keep her heart still, a move that left her balanced on one hand and two knees.

He was dressed in jeans and a short-sleeved Western shirt, and his gold-tone watch snatched a glimmer from the sunlight pouring through the window at his back. A silly notion that some kind of Norse sun god in cowboy clothing had come out of nowhere just to laugh at her brought her quickly to her feet.

"A person could say 'hello,' or 'yoo-hoo' or something, instead of creeping up on—"

"Hello." Chuckling, Trey hopped off the desk. "Yoo-hoo? Who says that?"

"Considerate people who aren't trying to scare the pants off…the life out of…"

"Your first instinct was better. I was tipi creepin'."

Refusing to be amused by that kind of a remark, Frankie swept a handful of construction paper scraps off the top of a pint-size desk, crumpled them into a ball and tossed it into the trash basket five feet away.

"Nice shot," Trey said. "You haven't lost your touch, Frankie. Boy, no wonder you have to start getting ready early." He peeked around the privacy screen for the reading nook, then checked out the cardboard writer's fortress. "Is this what they call a blackboard jungle?"

"They're learning centers. Haven't you ever noticed the way small children like to cozy up in a little cocoon sometimes? Like behind a chair or inside a big box."

He glanced at her, then at the small desk she was clearing of scissors and the yellow and blue letters she'd made. "Yeah, come to think of it. Tricia's like that."

She watched him file through his few memories of the daughter whose childhood he was missing as he turned away to examine her Magic Mathematician's Castle. "I built her a little playhouse. She helped me paint it. Pink and white. Those were her colors. I have trouble with the lighter values of red and green, so she got to pick out the paint."

No more larger-than-life Norse sun god. Trey Latimer was very much a man whose life was less than perfect. He missed someone. He touched the castle's pink satin pennant as though he were looking for something that might serve to patch a hole, and Frankie's heart stirred restlessly.

"Just a second. I have to shut this off." On hands and knees, she crawled back inside the tipi. The computer's green cursor winked at her. "Does it look kind of like a little fire in here?"

"Definitely. Well, more like a little fireball."

"No, I want it to look more like…" She emerged and found him leaning against the desk with arms folded across his chest, smiling wistfully. "You say the nicest things, Latimer," she said lightly. That sparkle in his eye made her stomach feel tingly, but she'd get over it. "You must really charm the females."

"Given half a chance." He braced his hands on the edge of the desk, preparing to lever himself up. "Want to go for a ride?"

"With you?" He nodded. "What have you got in mind?"

It was a foolish question. The mention of going for a ride evoked a bittersweet memory for her and probably the flip side of the same for him, whatever the flip side of bittersweet might be. But she was no longer a young girl with her heart pinned to her sleeve, and she could shrug off the memory with a knowing glance and a chuckle as easily as he could.

"Looking in on George," he said. "Among other things."

"To ask more questions?" She opened a cabinet door and sent the scissors clattering into a box of twenty more pairs. Whenever she went to see George, Lannie was there. The woman must have been saving up her vacation time for the past ten years, Frankie thought. Lannie left little for Frankie to do in George's presence except sit around and conjure up a raft of images of what might have happened that night. "I want to ask him, too, but I hate to upset him."

"Just to see what he might tell us, that's all." He shoved his hands into his pockets and crossed the floor in her direction. "Just to see George. Maybe snoop around the B.I.A. offices a little bit."

She brightened. "You mean investigate? Which offices?" This was all she really wanted from him, after all, and the fact that he was willing to include her was to his credit. She had to admit, he'd chalked up a point or two lately. "Do you think there's somebody over there who put somebody up to—"

"Hold on there, Watson. You're losing your *ABC*'s." He bent to pick up a paper letter that had fluttered to the floor. Straightening, he handed it to her. "You are a regular bloodhound, lady. I should have had you for a partner back when I was—"

She heard the word *lady* and wondered what he meant by it. Ladies were fancier than she was. Ladies were…

"Ancient history," he concluded. "You'd be a fossil by now, like me."

His cloudy gaze puzzled her. "A fossil? How old are you? Thirty-two?"

"Thirty-three. Cops age like dogs, though. One year equals seven."

"Oh, bull roar. You really look like a fossil."

There had never been anything antiquated about Trey Latimer. In fact, he still reminded her of the rock star pinups some of her friends had collected in high school. Frankie had never had time to waste on such fantasies. She had managed to wrangle a copy of Trey's senior picture from Luke, and she'd kept it on the table next to her bed long past the time when she could use adolescent foolishness as an excuse.

But the years had left their mark on everyone's heroes, rock stars and state champion all-stars alike. Absently Trey touched the scar above his right eye, smoothing his fingers over it as if to wipe it away.

"Are you okay?" she asked, more gently than she'd expected.

"Sure." His hand dropped away from his face, and he looked embarrassed. "I'm fine."

"Would it hurt if I touched it?" He shook his head, and his eyes turned catkin soft. She touched him gingerly with her fingertips as she tried to imagine what was beneath the seam of warm flesh, tried to detect the presence of something that didn't belong there. "I don't feel anything," she mused.

"I do." He offered a wry smile. "What do you think? Is it prickly?"

"Of course not." She took her hand away too quickly, as though the suggestion had made it so. "I thought this part of your head might be harder than the rest, but I guess that metal plate fit right in."

"You should have seen the damage I did to the bullet." He chuckled dryly. "Hell of a mess."

"Well, you sure don't look like a fossil." She closed the cupboard door, working the handles that didn't quite line up right. "The scar is kind of a nice touch. Before, you were almost too—"

His hand closed over hers just as the handle slipped into place. "Too what?"

His eyes reminded her of the river. Every mood, every shift of light, changed their shade. No one she loved had blue-grey eyes. They unnerved her. They were exotic and distant. Worse, they were hypnotic.

"Too beautiful," she said, even as she chided herself for being too honest.

He drew her hand behind his waist. She tugged a little, but his eyes were arresting, his smile reminiscent of his youthful charm. "Men aren't beautiful," he said quietly.

"Too good, then. You were almost too good…"

"To be true?"

"To be real. Except that you were Luke's friend, and that was real." She felt the curve of his spine against the back of her hand, and she swallowed. "That was *all* that was real."

"I thought so, too. Especially when you were suddenly too beautiful to be so young." He touched her temple with his thumb, tested the texture of the hair she'd swept back into her favorite single braid. "If I kiss you now, are we apt to get caught by the principal?"

She found voice to cover her shortness of breath with a little sauce. "Would that add to the excitement?"

He grinned. "It used to. Is he around?"

"He's a she, and she was here a little while ago."

He brushed her cheek with the back of his fingers and smiled regretfully. "Let's take a little walk down memory lane. I haven't seen the old school in years."

In Wakpala the elementary and high school classes all met in one old redbrick building, which was the tiny town's heartbeat. The echoing stairwells and dark hallways had an air of timelessness about them. Every step in every set of stairs was dished in the center, and the long tunnel of yellow and brown linoleum shone with the warm patina of fresh wax, yet to be scuffed by new school shoes. Frankie watched Trey peek into the rooms that, but for occasional refurbishing, had changed very little since he'd seen them last. She introduced the young teacher who was replacing Hope in the third grade. The few high school teachers Trey might have remembered weren't back in the classroom yet.

They strolled on, surprised by the way the smells of floor wax, mimeograph fluid and pine oil cleaner unlocked memories. Some of them had been made before her time or after his, but they both recalled the time the bats got into the boiler room and the day all the toilets in the boys' bathroom mysteriously overflowed at once.

But it was Trey's homecoming. Except for her years at the university, Frankie had never left. She suddenly saw herself as part of the same old woodwork.

"It's not very big, is it? It used to seem a lot bigger."

"When we were a lot littler." He sidled up to an unlabeled wooden door and gave her a mischievous grin. "Hey, this is an interesting room."

"That's the supply closet. It's always—" the doorknob turned in his hand "—not locked. Hmm."

"You know why?"

"Why?"

He pulled her into the room. She turned the light on. He shut the door. Shelves laden with reams of paper and pencils by the gross lined the narrow room from the floor to the fifteen-foot ceiling. He took a quick survey and nodded approvingly. "Because this is where Mr. Pease meets Miss Kuntz on his free period."

She shook her head quickly and wondered why he suddenly seemed so broad shouldered. "Neither one of them teaches here anymore."

"Small wonder." He reached for her hand. She watched him fondle her knuckles with his thumb, thinking she would tell him any time now to stop playing games.

Instead she volleyed as expected. "Anyway, how do you know?"

"I know because Mrs. Mohler sent me down here once for some typing paper."

"She gave you the key?" Her eyes narrowed playfully. "Were you teacher's pet, or what?"

"Some people thought I was trustworthy." She chortled at that, and so did he. The game, for the moment, was hard to resist. Time was playing funny tricks on their heads, and they were both back in school. "Changed my whole outlook on teachers that day," Trey recalled happily.

"What were they doing?"

"Acting like a couple of teenagers and loving it." He smiled as he reached back blindly for the light switch. Her tongue got tied up in the crazy throbbing in her throat, and she watched dumbly while he lowered the boom. "Stealing a kiss in the dark," he forewarned softly as he took her in his arms.

Oh, it was too deliciously sneaky, just like the night they'd parked by the river. Only now she could see even less of him and of herself and of what madness this was, because it was even darker, and the madness didn't show. She felt his hunger even before she tasted it on his lips. The heat that enveloped them seemed to seep in and curl up inside her, and she welcomed the soft stirring of his breath against her cheek. She breathed deeply of his woody, musky scent, and her equilibrium took flight. For balance, she put her arms around his waist.

She told herself to be prepared to fend him off, but there was a lack of conviction in the words. Fending off and floating didn't complement each other. Before she got tough, she wanted to wallow in this wonder of wonders for just a moment. She wanted Trey Latimer to kiss her.

And for a moment he made her believe she was the essence of his homecoming. He gathered her to him as though he had been waiting through the passage of time and all his trials just for this, and he gave her contained fire and controlled light. He had saved them for her. Her lips parted for the entrance of his tongue, and she thrilled to the easy pressure of his clothed chest against her sheathed nipples. Just that much, she told herself wildly. Just the taste of temptation. Savor that and no more.

He rubbed her back in slow, dizzying circles as he turned his head to sip at the corner of her mouth and trace its shape with the tip of his tongue. There was no assault, no test of strength. Only the sweetest, warmest invitation. He kissed her until she was ready to deny herself thought, dignity, even her next breath in favor of a whole feast of him.

Just the taste, and no more.

She was no green girl this time. She knew she could not safely get her fill. She had learned that there was no such thing. She returned one soft, conclusive kiss, then ducked under his arm, flipped the light back on and cracked open the door. She knew the damp sheen on his face and the heat in his eyes must have been a match for what he saw as he looked at her.

"It's too hot to breathe in here," she said more steadily than she'd expected to. He smiled knowingly and drew a long, slow breath.

Hard-soled shoes clicked against the linoleum just outside the door. They exchanged a quick look of panic before Trey turned to scan the shelves. The doorknob slid from Frankie's hand.

"There's the stuff I need, Trey." She pointed to a lofty shelf just as the door swung open. "Can you reach that roll of yellow paper?" Then she turned and acknowledged Theresa No Heart. "Uh-oh. Caught red-handed by the principal."

The short, stocky, hawk-faced woman was not amused. "Did I leave this door unlocked?"

"Yes, and lucky for me, because I have one more bulletin board to finish," Frankie said easily. "Theresa, have you met Sheriff Latimer? He's looking for the man who beat up George."

Trey smiled and offered a handshake, which Theresa accepted coolly. "Good. I hope you find him." She eyed each of them briefly as she backed out the door. "Thought some kids were back already, getting into stuff. Be sure you sign a requisition, Frances."

"I'll leave it in your mailbox."

But the woman was already halfway down the hall. They stared at each other again. Trey looked even more sheepish than Frankie felt, and she giggled. "Cat got your tongue?"

He rolled his eyes. "Friendly sort, isn't she?"

"She's hard to fool. She's been in this business a

long time." She folded her arms across her chest and cocked a warning eyebrow. "So don't try anything else."

"Watch it, Frances. Your face'll start to look like hers." Smiling roguishly, he jerked a thumb toward the high shelf. "You really need that stuff?"

"I'm not walking out of here without it."

He shouldered the long roll of paper like a rifle, and they exchanged conspiratorial smiles as they continued their walk down the hall.

Frankie felt good about taking this ride with Trey Latimer. The Dakota sun was riding high. Flanking the highway on both sides, the bright yellow faces of cultivated sunflowers followed the sunlight like earthbound ducklings, turning and yearning after their mama. Frankie extended her arm out the window and imagined running her hand over their heads as the pickup flew past.

She refused to think that this feeling was like old times, when he'd favored her with his attention and she'd been full of herself just because of it. That kind of naiveté went by the boards with a little experience. A woman remembered that the long ride home after the Homecoming party had been sweet, had made a young girl's heart sing and had been the last time she was favored by him. Until now. But now that she was a woman, she had wisdom on her side. She would rely on that and remember that the old feelings, as light and as heavy as they were, had belonged to a young girl. She was safe from them now. She'd just proven that to herself.

Even so, she reached for the yellow sun faces, which was a girlish thing to do. Her left hand was suddenly enveloped in the warmth of his. She turned her face from the wind to glance first at their hands, clasped in the middle of the pickup seat, then at his face. His hair had drifted over his forehead, and his eyes were smiling.

"What'll you do if you catch a grasshopper?" he asked.

"Put it in your bait box, Latimer." She laughed as she drew her arm back into the cab. "I want you to keep on fishing until you finally get a bite."

Trey laughed. He was an experienced fisherman, and he knew damn well when the prize was game.

Standing Rock Agency Superintendent Bill Curly was a cagey sort, in the tradition of Bureau employees. They were well versed in the art of passing the buck. Frankie had claimed to be the hunter on their team and she knew what that entailed. Buck hunting was never easy in the maze of B.I.A. red tape, but for her people, it had become a way of life. A poor substitute for the traditional hunt, but those bucks were there somewhere. Those answers. Those people in power. Those decisions nobody ever seemed to want to make. The good hunter flushed them out.

Frankie introduced Trey, and he signaled her to let him take the lead. Curly offered them a seat in his well-ordered brown-and-green office.

"I'm following up on a couple of ideas in connection with George Tracker's case," Trey began. "We were just going over to see George, but I was wondering—"

"I understand George has come out of his coma." Curly offered Frankie a rubber-lipped smile. "I know you're relieved."

She returned an icy stare. "His problems aren't over, Mr. Curly."

"These things take time, don't they?" Curly's chair creaked as he leaned back. "And I'm sure our Bureau police will find the man who's responsible for it."

These things take time. How many times had Frankie heard that one lately, and from how many people? Curly had nearly colorless eyes, bloodless skin, and there was no reassurance in the tone of his voice, no matter what words he said. They were all alike, these bureaucrats. She glanced at Trey, whose expression was unreadable.

Trey lifted one finger to push his straw hat another inch above his eyebrows and proceeded with his business. "I've been working with Two Hawk on this. Covering all the bases between his jurisdiction and mine, so to speak. I wonder if you could tell me how government contracts for reservation projects are assigned. Who reviews the bids?"

Curly frowned. "You mean, what? Construction contracts?"

"Like the housing projects."

The back of his desk chair followed Curly forward as he straightened. "This has something to do with George Tracker?"

"I don't know yet. George was trying to get into business with another guy, and I'm just following the paper trail."

"Good luck," Frankie muttered.

Curly glanced at Frankie, then folded his hands and rocked them back and forth as though his wrists needed exercise. His mouth was the only part of his face that made a pretense of smiling. "Yessir, with the B.I.A. that can be quite a job. Most of those decisions are made by the area office in Aberdeen, but they have to be approved in D.C. Sometimes, if it's a major project—"

"Who would I see in Aberdeen?" Trey asked.

"Are you any relation to Phillip Latimer?"

Trey lifted his chin and gave himself a moment before giving the man a response. "His son."

"That's what I thought," Curly mused. "I thought I'd heard that the new sheriff was the same Latimer."

"His son," Trey repeated, his voice deadly soft. "Not the same."

"Well, you might try Richard White. Now, he's in finance, but he'd love to tell you all the ifs, ands and buts, show you how much he knows and get you totally confused." Curly's pale brows shot up as his whole face seemed to broaden in an eerie, self-satisfied grin. "Good luck pinning him down on anything that's pending, though."

Good luck pinning any of these civil servants down on anything, Trey thought. What he needed was an FBI badge. But he offered a parting handshake. "I'm interested in finding out how it all works," he said. "I can wade through the jargon."

"We," Frankie intoned with a pointed glance at Trey. *"We* are wondering how it all works."

"Well, George must know, if he's taking the big business plunge," Curly said as he held his office door open for them.

"George still has some recovering to do," Frankie said.

Emma Tracker was dozing in a chair in the corner of George's room when Trey and Frankie walked in. Her chin rested comfortably in the round white collar of her flowered cotton dress, while her ample bosom was tucked in the cradle of her folded arms. The shades were drawn, and Trey felt like an intruder. If they hadn't come nearly fifty miles for this visit, he would have turned around and tiptoed out again. A tender place inside him ached as he watched Frankie bend close to her mother and gently wake the woman. When had Emma aged so much? he wondered.

"How is he, Mama?" Frankie asked. "Any change?"

Emma sat up and wiped the corner of her eye with the side of her finger. "They're sending him up to Bismarck for some tests. Maybe tomorrow, they said." She tipped her head to one side, and Frankie stepped out of the way. "Is that you, Trey?"

"Yes, ma'am. It's been—"

Emma straightened her dress with one hand as she stood up and waved him into the middle of the room. Her bright giggle sent his awkwardness flying. "I've told you before, sonny, it's 'Mom.' None of this 'ma'am' like those ol' farm boys say."

Trey bent to kiss Emma's weathered cheek and let her pat his shoulders. "You're about the only Tracker I haven't run into since I've been back."

"Well, you're not supposed to run into me," she grumbled good-naturedly. "You're supposed to come to my house and see me. I can't be running around so much like you young folks."

"Mama's practicing up to act like an old grandma before her first grandchild is even born," Frankie explained.

"My children are holdin' out on me." Emma sighed and wagged her graying head. "If George plans to do anything about it with your sister, I told him he'd better hurry up and get on with it. She's not gettin' any younger, that girl."

"None of us is," Trey admitted with a chuckle.

"They say you're tryin' to find out who did this to my boy." Emma jerked her chin in the direction of the bed.

Frankie moved closer to the bedside, and Trey nodded as he glanced over and saw that George was stirring. "They say you know all about police work," Emma added.

The elder woman's hopeful tone disturbed him. "I'm just trying to help out," Trey muttered as he moved to assume the post opposite Frankie at George's bedside.

"How's it goin', Gorgeous?" he asked as he pulled up a chair, braced his hands on the backrest and sat astraddle.

"Can't see. My right eye's no good." Trey noted that his speech was considerably clearer, and his color was better. "An' my left side's kinda goofy."

"You mean you're only half goofy now?" Frankie teased.

Trey glanced up and tagged his grin to hers. George responded with a feeble, "Ayyy," which meant, go on. With a glance and a nod, Frankie encouraged Trey to go on. So he did.

"Can you remember anything about how you got hit, George? Was it a truck?"

"No." George rolled his head, as if in slow motion, from side to side. "Don't remember no truck."

"A man?"

"I think…" Thinking took a moment. George licked his lips. His brow furrowed. "Must have been a man."

"You were in Mobridge," Trey reminded him gently, and George nodded. "Main Street?" The unbandaged eye registered nothing. "After Lannie left, did you go back to your pickup?"

"Where's my pickup?" he asked, suddenly concerned.

"It's at home, George," Frankie said. "We brought it home. But the night you got hurt, it was parked on Main Street. Remember that?"

George lifted his hand toward the tray table and the

plastic jug of water that stood there. The ice rattled as Frankie poured him a glass.

"I want to find the man who hit you, George," Trey said. He remembered Luke's request, and the way Emma had made him sound like the great white hope. God help him, he surely wasn't that. But he looked up and saw some kind of hope in Frankie's eyes, too. Maybe not great, and it had nothing to do with the fact that he was white. But he had one thing going for him. If nothing else, he knew how to follow the trail and ask the right questions.

He turned back to his friend's battered face. "I *will* find him for you, but you'll have to help me. Tell me whether you'd ever seen him before."

George licked his lips.

"Was he tall or short?"

George nodded.

Frankie held the glass of water near George's chin and pressed the end of a plastic straw against his lips, scolding Trey while George drank. "You're confusing him. He's trying to remember, but you're—"

Trey patted George's shoulder. "Don't worry about it, George. It'll come back to you. You're going into the construction business, right? Remember Craig Pratt?"

"Craig Pratt." George released the straw as he lifted his hand and made his right thumb and forefinger into a circle. "Little John Lennon glasses."

"Yeah, that's the guy." And this was how it worked. Trey exchanged a knowing glance with Frankie's less certain one. Bit by bit, it would start coming back. "You worked for him before."

"Worked on a house."

"That's right," Trey assured him. "You'll work on

more houses. Mr. Pratt said to tell you he wants you back on the job as soon as you're better."

"Going to Bismarck for tests." George smiled wistfully at Frankie. "Hope I can pass."

"You're doing fine." Trey turned to Emma, who was standing at the foot of the bed. "I really think he's doing great."

"Wish you could go to the powwow down in Bullhead this weekend, Gorgeous," Frankie said. She offered more water, but he turned away. "All the girls sure miss your fancy dancing. Remember how you used to fancy dance?"

"Gave my bustles away."

"Well, you quit dancing a few years back, but now you ought to think about getting back to it when you get well. Kick up your heels again." She set the glass aside. "I'll ask Daddy to make you a new set of bustles. I'll be dancing this weekend. I'll be dancing for you, because you're getting better."

"Next time," George said. "Tell them I'll be there next time." Then he smiled and whispered, "Frankie."

Frankie swallowed the lump in her throat once she and Trey were outside the room. George knew her. That was progress.

"He's trying so hard," she said, and then she remembered a rebuttal she'd filed away for Trey. "Craig Pratt wasn't wearing glasses."

"He had them in his pocket." Trey patted his own empty shirt pocket. "In a case. Don't tell me you missed that, Watson." He slipped his arm around her shoulders, and neither of them questioned the ease with which they fell into step together. "It's coming back slowly, Frankie, but it's coming back."

There and then, as they walked down the hospital corridor, Frankie decided that she was going back to visit Craig Pratt. It was kind of a shady idea—not one she wanted to share with Trey just yet—but if there was any way she could help Pratt stay in the running for those contracts, then for George's sake, she would see what she could do.

Besides that, there were bucks lurking somewhere, maybe in the pages of those contracts. Big bucks. And they had to be flushed out somehow.

Chapter 7

Trey had tried to catch Frankie by phone before she left for the powwow in Bullhead, but he'd missed her. He wanted to tell her about his call to the Aberdeen Area Office and the appointment he'd set up. Actually it was more than that. He figured if he told her about the appointment, she would want to go along with him. He'd wanted to see if he had her figured right.

But she'd already left. He had no choice but to go looking for her. If he remembered right, these Indian dances were usually whole weekend affairs, and the little town of Bullhead, which he'd had occasion to visit maybe once in his life, was way the hell out in the sticks. As long as he'd lived on the reservation, he'd never actually been to a powwow, even though he'd seen some of the dances demonstrated at ball games and rodeos. He and Luke had taken in many of the small Indian rodeos when they were growing up, but Luke had never invited him to a powwow.

Maybe he didn't have such a great reason now. He was headed for her turf—an unfamiliar Indian enclave within the white world of the Dakotas. Most South Dakotans steered clear of towns like Bullhead. Not that he'd been one of them, but you had to have reason to be there, didn't you? He might not fit in. He was about to turn himself into a sore thumb, and people were bound to look him over and wonder why the county sheriff was butting into their celebration. Frankie might even wonder. What if he told her that he planned to head for Aberdeen on Monday, and she said, So? He would feel like a damn fool.

He went over it in his head as he tooled along the gravel road, trying to turn the piece of news into something really good. He could say it wasn't every day that the head of finance agreed to take time out of his busy schedule. He could tell her how this guy had started tripping over his tongue when Trey had identified himself, and maybe that meant something. He wasn't sure whether it was the word *sheriff* or the Latimer name that had rattled the bureaucrat, but it smelled like some kind of collusion.

Maybe it wasn't a scoop worth stopping the presses for, but it was enough to send him careening across the prairie in search of a local tradition that had never drawn him out of his way before. Indian dancing. What the hell, it wasn't Indian dancing; it was *Frankie* dancing. All of a sudden he was willing to drive to hell and back just to watch Frankie Tracker dance.

Pretty little Frankie with the sparkling brown eyes. Lately he'd been letting himself get lost in those eyes.

It gave him a strange feeling to look at her now and remember the same eyes in the face of his best friend's tomboyish kid sister. He didn't know exactly when all that had changed so dramatically, so beautifully, but he remembered the night it had hit him. Hit him hard. He hadn't been much more than a kid himself, and control had usually been a matter of somebody's mother walking in and asking if anyone wanted anything to eat yet. He'd nearly blown it that night when he'd somehow ended up parked by the river with the little girl who'd suddenly hopped into a woman's body.

But she wasn't a little girl anymore.

The sun was sinking toward the rim of the bowl of flat-topped ridges that sheltered the little town. It was even smaller than Wakpala, but then, Wakpala was different. Even though the population of the town was predominantly Indian, Wakpala had a public school—*his* old school—and the railroad had once run a depot there. Bullhead was one of the smaller, isolated Indian communities where people still spoke Lakota, which was a foreign language to Trey.

Nevertheless, it was a pretty town. From the hilltop Trey could see the scattering of little houses, the metal building that served as a community center and the network of narrow gravel roads. Gnarled scrub oaks lined the banks of meandering Rock Creek, and in the midst of one of the groves stood a couple of tipis and an array of drab army tents, along with a number of blue or yellow weekend campers. Here and there a white wisp of smoke puffed at the treetops, and the steady drumbeat seemed to reverberate along the valley floor.

Trey lit a cigarette and chuckled into his own cloud of smoke when he noticed the carnival rides set up in a clearing beyond the camp. It was one of those traveling shows with mostly kiddie rides, a Tilt-A-Whirl too small to provide any thrills but big enough to make you upchuck your corn dogs, and a fair-sized Ferris wheel at the center of it all. Great contrast, he thought as he swung the pickup onto the narrow, rutted approach.

He parked in a grassy spot alongside a cluster of vehicles, got out, shut the door and braced his forearm along the top of the cab. Then he peered over the roof, ostensibly taking time to finish his cigarette. He never walked into an unfamiliar scene without sizing it up first to see how he'd fit. How many times had he driven by an empty bowery? This was the first time he'd seen one of the traditional Indian dance arenas—basically a ring of plank benches sheltered by a willow thatch on poles—actually in use. Its open center was filled with costumed dancers, who were stomping up a small storm on the resilient prairie sod. A flagpole shot up from the very center, and the Stars and Stripes fluttered above the whole doings.

Maybe he wasn't totally out of place. That was his flag, too. And somewhere in that crowd there was a woman who lured him whenever he saw her and, lately, lured him just as strongly even when she was out of sight. He needed to find her, and if she wanted him there, he would stay awhile. If not, well… He jerked the pickup door open and disposed of the cigarette butt in the ashtray. Obviously if she didn't want him here, he wouldn't stick around.

Besides feeling uneasy, he felt stupid for feeling uneasy. Hell, he'd walked into places where people greeted him with loaded guns. All he wanted to do here was talk to a woman. Talk to her. That was all he had in mind. He didn't need the local council's approval for that.

He looked around for someone he might know. One
face seemed familiar—he thought maybe he'd known
the man in the Mount Rushmore T-shirt and the Kist
livestock cap in some other life. He nodded. The man
nodded back, took a long pull on his can of orange pop
and turned away. Trey decided he had a poor memory;
he'd been gone a long time, and he didn't know anybody
anymore. And he sure as hell didn't belong here.

*Find the woman and have a talk. That's all you're
here for.*

From the announcer's stand at the far side of the
bowery came the call over the loudspeaker for "little
boys' fancy dancers." The men and women were leaving
the circle just as Trey walked up, and the little boys were
straggling in. Parents and grandparents were adjusting
the dance bells that were tied to the children's legs and
fixing the porcupine hair roachs so that they bristled on
top of their little heads.

"Let's hurry every chance we get, now, folks," the announcer said patiently. "*Hoka! Hoka!* Preliminaries for
little boys' fancy dance." Several thunks on the bass
drum punctuated the call.

The smell of boiled beef and fat-fried dough made
the juices roil in Trey's stomach, but he saw no food.
He was going to ask someone where he might find
Frankie, but the drum was revving up, and the singers'
high-pitched chant distracted him. He'd heard the music
before, of course, on television or in the school gym.
Never in a such a natural context, sung as it was meant
to be. Or maybe he had, and he'd just never paid any attention. The bowery and the tawny hills and the smell
of meat cooking mesmerized him. And two dozen little
boys suddenly turned into whirling dervishes, their

feathered bustles, beadwork and breech clouts providing a kaleidoscope of color.

Trey found himself nearly as interested in watching the children dance as he was in finding an even vaguely familiar face. He moved closer, breeching the outer circle. Damn, those kids were cute. He liked kids. He liked kid stuff, like all those little nooks and crannies Frankie had built for her classroom. He missed having kid stuff around him. He missed watching Tricia pretend to be a ballerina, hearing her sing the new songs she'd learned in school and tasting the chocolate milk she liked to make. She would have been all eyes and ears, watching these kids dance.

He reached for his cigarettes again.

"Did you eat?"

"Did I—" He glanced quickly over his shoulder and found an older woman staring at him. She was flanked by a long table, several cardboard boxes and a couple of large kettles. Now he knew where the smell was coming from.

"I didn't see you go through the line," she said. "Did you miss the feed?"

"I just got here."

"There's still plenty," the round-faced woman said as she lifted the lid off a kettle of soup. "You can eat something before they take it back to the kitchen."

"Thanks," Trey said. "I'm fine." He didn't see anything handy to put the soup in, and he didn't want to put the lady to any trouble. But it felt good to be asked. "I'm looking for Frankie Tracker."

"She was around here." The woman squinted as she surveyed the confines of the bowery. "They'll be having the women's fancy dance pretty quick, so maybe she's getting ready." She pointed to an urn at the end of the table. "There's coffee."

"Thank you." She was still looking at him expectantly. He smiled. "Sure, I'll have some."

The woman produced a cup from one box, then plunged her hand into another one. "You could use a piece of frybread, too, couldn't you?"

"I could sure use a piece of frybread." Trey grinned as he accepted the offering with one hand and reached into his pocket with the other. "How much do I owe you?"

"This is a powwow. Everybody eats." The woman filled the cup with hot, rich black coffee and handed it to him. "No charge."

He should have known better. This woman could have been Emma Tracker's sister. If you didn't eat, there was something wrong. And when you did eat, you felt better. You thought of things to talk about, and you laughed easier.

The last bite of the square piece of fried dough was halfway into his mouth when he saw Frankie across the bowery. He filled his mouth, chewed slowly and watched her make her way around the circle. She stopped to speak to another woman, then stopped again to admire a little girl's satin costume. Trey didn't think she'd seen him yet. He rested his shoulder against a pole and stood in the shadows of the leafy shelter, sipping his coffee. If she continued walking in the same direction, she would plow right in to him. The prospect delighted him.

She wore a satin dress and carried a shawl trimmed with long, fluid fringe, all in white. She was dazzling in white, but her beaded hair strings, belt, leggings and moccasins were a bold counterpoint of primary colors, which he was able to discern, and crisp geometric designs. Her black braids glistened as she strode through the wild grass with royal bearing.

Then she looked his way, deliberately, as though she'd been aware of him all along. It felt as if he'd just turned his face to the sun as the smile that started in her eyes spread to his extremities. And suddenly he was in the right place at the right time. He straightened and drained his cup, watching her all the while as she approached.

"You look terrific," he said, by way of greeting her.

"And you look surprised." She adjusted her shawl and looked up at him. He could have sworn he detected a hint of coyness beneath those long black lashes.

"I'm not surprised. I'm just…"

"Wondering what happened to my usual jeans?"

"Actually I'm just looking. Enjoying what I see." She had him, and she knew it. And he was enjoying that, too. "Is that okay?"

"Sure. Are you being a tourist in your own backyard this weekend?"

"I heard you tell George about the powwow, and I thought I'd come check it out." He turned his attention back to the activity inside the circle. The music had stopped, and the boys were anxiously watching three men who were obviously scoring them. "Is this a contest?"

"It is if you're entered up, which I'm not this time out. But my sisters are." She waved to someone behind him. He turned to see two young girls, one dressed in blue, the other in lemon-yellow dance finery. They were both younger versions of Frankie.

"Remember…" Frankie began, and Trey smiled at them. How well he remembered. "No, you wouldn't remember Sweetie and Crystal. Sweetie's ten, and Crystal's twelve." She turned to the girls. "This is Trey Latimer. He's Lannie's brother." And to Trey she announced proudly, "Sweetie won twenty-five dollars in the little girls' shawl dance."

"Hey, that must've been some dance for that kind of money," he praised as he shook Sweetie's hand.

Sweetie nodded, but Crystal had bigger fish to fry. "Can we go to the carnival now?"

"Did you eat?" The girls nodded in unison. "Go on, then, but change your clothes." Frankie's permission had the effect of a dismissal bell.

She turned to Trey. "Did you eat?"

He lifted his empty cup. "That seems to be the question of the hour."

"You need more than coffee. This is a powwow." She was moving toward the long table. The coffee and some of the boxes were still there. "I'll get you some frybread. You like frybread, don't you?"

"Love it." He would have loved whatever it was that smelled like beef even more.

When it was Frankie's turn to dance, Trey slid back into the shadows and nibbled at a piece of cold frybread while he watched. The costumes were spectacular, each one with its own color scheme and character. Sequins, satin, beads and fringe were the vogue, with lengths of satin ribbon fluttering like small pennants. As the rhythm picked up, the colors swirled faster.

Frankie was magnificent. Her shawl draped over the arms she held akimbo, she spun like a top, wheeling the long fringe around her in the way of all women twirling in finery. Her feet skimmed the grass with a heel, toe, heel, pirouette, toe, heel in answer to the drum's insistent demands. The beaded leggings covered her calves, but once in a while, during a spin, Trey was treated to a glimpse of shapely knee.

The song ended abruptly, and the women dispersed, some shaking their heads, others adjusting belts or folding shawls. Frankie's face glowed, flushed and damp from her performance.

"Oh, what a workout. The drummers caught me," she told Trey as she shook her shawl and folded it, brushing the fringe into line. "Did you see that? I took another whole step after the last beat."

"That's bad?"

"It would be if I had a number." She smiled and showed him her back and the absence of a contestant number. "I'm just dancing for George. You know, celebrating." Invigorated, she grabbed his arm and squeezed a grin out of him as she repeated, "Celebrating, Latimer. Did you come to celebrate?"

"Sure," he said, laughing. "Mostly by watching you dance. You were terrific."

"I look terrific. I dance terrific," she said as they left the bowery together. "Tonight's my night. Later I'll dance again. Traditional, this time. I like that better because—" she wiped her hand across her forehead and made a production of catching her breath "—it doesn't play me out so much."

"Does that mean no carnival rides?"

"Do you want to?" They were already heading in that direction. "Just the Ferris wheel. That's the only one I really like."

Her zeal was infectious, and Trey felt a new bounce in his own step as they threaded their way past the men's fancy dancers, who were gathering for their entry.

"Didn't I hear somebody order a change of clothes first?" he teased.

"I'm in charge, so I get to be the exception to my rules," she declared, patting her own chest. "It's just the girls and me this weekend. We've set up our camp, and we're here to dance and eat and take in the carnival and—"

"Celebrate."

"Celebrate." She smiled up at him, her eyes creating a bright spot in the evening shadows. "I'm glad you came."

"Me, too."

Taken together, the Ferris wheel and the Tilt-A-Whirl reminded Trey of a pair of the feathered dance bustles he'd just seen the men wearing. They picked their way through a sparse stand of oaks, passing two boys who were laughingly chasing a third, telling him to "wait up." Trey bought tickets—more than they would need, but they were a bargain in quantity—and they hurried to get in line for the next spin.

The cars rocked and rolled each time the big wheel stopped, and the ticket taker offered the same admonition each time he pushed the safety bar in place over a group of children's laps. "No rocking." When Trey handed him a pair of tickets, he did a double take and shook his head. "Don't rock the boat, big guy."

The first thing he did was put his arm around Frankie. That was part of what Ferris wheels were all about. She smiled, and he figured he was doing just fine. The wheel turned, and they rose, up, up into the painted sky. Down below, the laughter of children was punctuated by the steady thumping of the dance drum. They passed the treetops and greeted the setting sun.

Trey's breath caught in his chest when he felt her hand on his thigh.

"It feels like we're traveling the way the sun goes," Frankie said. He smiled and drew her closer. "Up, over the world, and down again, while the moon is sailing around the opposite way."

"The moon's coming up behind us." He swiveled toward her and glanced back, pitching their feet higher. "See?"

"Oh, no, don't lean back," she warned. But she laughed, unafraid to have fun with him. "You're rocking the boat, big guy."

"Come here," he said, gathering her even closer and hoping her hand might slide back just an inch or two. "Hold me still."

The wheel made its rounds several times, and he watched the feather fluff on her hair strings flutter as the breeze played with a wisp of hair that had come loose by her cheek. They were heading for the top of the world when the ride slowed down.

"If it stops at the top—"

"I get to kiss you," he said.

"I was going to say, we'll be able to see the whole—"

The chair swayed as they rolled to a stop. He watched her as he dipped his head, watched for the lashes to lower and the nose to rise. He pressed his lips against hers and felt the warmth of her breath fill him. Her fingers stirred on his thigh and made his skin burn beneath his jeans. His arms were filled with satin and warm flesh, and he tasted the sweet honey of her mouth with a greedy tongue as they hovered, suspended in time above God's country. When his lips released hers, she looked up at him. The wonder that filled her eyes seeped into his chest and expanded it tenfold.

"—sky," she finished finally. "We're part of the sunset."

"You look wonderful, Frankie." He ducked to touch that fascinating wisp of hair with his nose and whisper, "So beautiful."

"Everything looks beautiful from a Ferris wheel," she said.

Disembarking was a shaky business for both of them.

He offered her another ride, but she shook her head. She looked a little dreamy-eyed, and he had a pretty good idea what she needed. He knew damn well what *he* needed. But they would wait. The ache was almost as delicious as the thought of easing it.

From somewhere in the crowd a scruffy little brown-eyed boy appeared and tugged on Frankie's dress. She ruffled his mop of black hair.

"Brandon, were you just riding the Ferris wheel, too?" The boy nodded, grinning broadly. Frankie turned and touched Trey's arm. "Trey, this is Brandon Crow Feather. He was in my class last year."

"Hi, Brandon."

The boy looked Trey over. "Are you gonna marry my teacher?"

Frankie laughed easily. "Trey is my friend, Brandon. You guys have to stop worrying about getting me a husband."

"He's your boyfriend, huh?"

"He's the sheriff, Brandon. You'd better not make him mad."

Trey laughed, totally destroying his potential to inspire fear, and handed the boy a ticket. "You wanna ride the Ferris wheel again, Brandon?"

"Are you gonna ride again?" Brandon asked.

"Why?"

"'Cause I wanna get the seat behind yours so I can watch you guys."

Frankie groaned, and Trey greased Brandon's palm with more tickets before the boy skipped away.

"All last year those kids kept after me," Frankie said as they headed back through the oak grove toward the campground. "'When are you gonna get married?' they'd say. 'My sister is having a baby, Miss Tracker. You should have a baby.' They sounded like my mother."

"Who wants grandchildren," Trey recalled. He shoved his hands into his pockets and smiled slowly. "So when *are* you going to get married? Got any prospects?"

"I'm not looking for prospects. That's what every-body around here does. Get married, have kids." She shrugged. "Or have kids, get married. Or just have kids."

"That's what a lot of people do in a lot of places."

"Not me. Not till I'm good and ready. It's too easy to make a mistake these days."

She left him standing outside her tent to contemplate mistakes easily made, and he was trying to decide whether either or both of them were supposed to be in the process of making one when she called for him.

She stood in the center under the tent's peak. Her satin outfit was folded and placed in one side of a suitcase that lay open at her feet on the canvas floor. His gaze trailed from the suitcase to the beaded toes of her moccasins to the eight-inch fringe at the bottom of her elkskin dress. The home-tanned leather was the color of antique ivory. Long fringe cascaded from the butterfly sleeves and rustled softly as she wrapped her braids with strips of white fur. Like rows of corn, the intricate beadwork covered the sleeves and the yoke in white with colorful geometric patterns. She dressed by the light of a kerosene lamp, casting long shadows on the tent walls.

Trey felt as though he'd been sucked back in time.

She knew his thoughts. She saw the wonder in his eyes. "It was my grandmother's dress," she said. "Your sister has her spool bed. I have this dress."

"It's beautiful. It looks like something from a museum."

"That's because that's where most of the old ones are," she said as she wove a beaded hair string into the second fur wrap. "Or else they're kept in collections belonging to rich white people. My grandmother made this dress for making celebrations. She gave it to me when I was a little girl and told me to grow into it and dance for her. And I do. For her memory." She tied a piece of downy fluff at the bottom of her braid wrap and let it fall against her breast with a self-satisfied smile. "But I've said I'm honoring George's return to us with this dance tonight."

She lifted a hair-pipe breastplate from her suitcase and held it up to her shoulders. The ivory network of long, slender bone beads strung horizontally on sturdy thongs clickity-clacked as it fell past her knees, as though she had released the catch on a Venetian blind.

"This gets heavy," she commented as she lined the ties up at the back of her neck.

"Let me help." He moved behind her, reached over her shoulders and took the weight of the breastplate in his hands. "You're going to dance in this? I'll bet your outfit weighs more than you do."

"Almost. That's why traditional dancing is pretty sedate." She put on a beaded brow band and cinched a wide belt around her waist before turning for his assessment. "How do I look?"

"Mystical." With two fingers he touched the nubbly beadwork on her shoulder, then lifted one fur-wrapped braid and let it slide through the tunnel his hand made. The powder-soft winter beaver soothed his palm. "But earthy," he added as he cupped her cheek in his hand. "This is how it feels to look at you."

He kissed her softly, his lips eddying over hers to tantalize, the way her exotic beauty tempted him, teased him with a stinging hunger to learn every secret she covered with such heavy protection. Just as softly, her lips parted for him, and she greeted his tongue with the tentative touch of the tip of her own. She sighed against his lips, and he kissed her again, then brushed her lips with two gentle fingers.

"This could be one of those mistakes-made-easy if we don't watch it," she said. Her lingering gaze spoke of hunger, but when he laid his hands on her shoulders, she ducked away, bending to take a buckskin pouch from her suitcase. The breastplate swayed like a beaded curtain.

"Kissing me isn't going to ruin your life, Frankie." He shoved his hands into his pockets, cursing his itching palms as he watched her draw a clutch of eagle feathers from the pouch. Their quill tips were bound in buckskin and beads. "Does that go in your hair?"

"It's a fan. Women don't wear eagle feathers. At least, they didn't traditionally." She wagged the bottom of her braid in front of his face and smiled. "They can wear the feather fluff, like this."

"Some feminists might object to associating fluff with women," he said, smiling, too, because she could

not hide that dreamy-eyed look, and because he knew
he'd put it there.

"Well, some traditionals don't approve of the
women's fancy dance. In the old days women—" She
threw back the tent flap and invited him to follow her.
"You'll see the difference."

The drumbeat was pervasive. The bowery was illu-
minated by floodlights, and the benches beneath the
thatched shelter were packed with people. Outside the
structure, the prairie grass had been worn down by a
continual procession of social strollers, young and old,
circling the bowery. Children chased each other, darting
around and ducking behind taller bodies. Raw-boned
dogs sniffed at cast-off paper wrappers.

The announcer called for the women's traditional
dancers, and Frankie took her place in the circle of women
within the circle of the bowery within the circle of the
footpath. Trey, too, felt enclosed and included as he braced
his shoulders against one of the bowery's support poles
and watched as the women in traditional dress expressed
the rhythm of the drum by bouncing primly at the knee,
their feet barely moving. Some carried a shawl over one
arm, some held arms akimbo, but all of them held their
heads high and their shoulders perfectly square. Now and
then Frankie was moved to wave her fan, as though signaling to the left, then right, then above her head.

Trey couldn't imagine how those who were compet-
ing might be judged. The circle struck him as a sister-
hood, a statement of feminine dignity. The women were
earthbound through their feet and connected with one
another through the circle. He saw nothing competitive
in it, but it was surely something for a man to admire.
There were no ruffles and few hints of the gray shade

he recognized as pink, but the feminine strength in the circle—the age and the youth, the wisdom and the in-experience—was humbling.

The whole circle was beautiful, as were its parts. The way Frankie shone under the lights made him shiver. His heart pounded along with the drumbeat, cele-brating not only her striking beauty, but the timelessness of that beauty.

And the fact that she was not a little girl anymore.

When the dance was over, she left the circle. Again she looked left and right, searching the crowd. Trey stepped away from the pole and offered her a welcoming smile.

"I've donated to the singers for an honoring song." She reached for his hand, and it occurred to him that the dance had revived her. "You know, because Gorgeous is back with us again. I want you to lead it with me."

He felt chosen and dumbfounded, both at once. "But I don't know—"

She squeezed his hand. "Just take slow steps and stay beside me. We've had to work to complicate our dances. They used to be for everyone." Her eyes teased him. "Even big, stubborn cops."

All of a sudden he was out there in the middle of it all, with everyone watching. "If we hold hands, they'll be talking about it for a month," Frankie muttered by way of explanation as she drew her hand away. "But stay close to my side."

Hell, he wasn't about to stray.

She showed him the simple hesitation step as the singers swung into a slow, dignified song. All around them, people came to their feet, and many of them queued behind them as they took a slow turn around the bowery, moving as a couple. Crystal and Sweetie came running from behind the announcer's stand and joined Frankie and Trey at the front of the line. By the time it was over, the outer circle of people had become an inner circle.

And when it was over, he, too, was renewed.

Frankie's sisters followed them outside the bowery. "We're gonna ride some more," Crystal said.

"Do you have tickets left?" Trey asked. He took a handful from the breast pocket of his blue chambray shirt. "Here's a few more. And here's…"

Frankie stayed his hand from producing his billfold. "Cool it, Latimer. They'll go all night."

"We're celebrating, aren't we?" He turned to the two bright young faces. "Aren't we, girls?" The two grinning faces nodded vigorously, and the girls accepted Trey's money. "Are you hungry? How about—" The nods turned negative as the girls scampered away.

"I'll bet you're the one who's hungry," Frankie told Trey as she watched her sisters dart around an old woman.

"I'm fine." He laid a possessive hand at the base of her neck. "How about you? How are you holding up under all that weight?"

"I'd like to unload a few pounds," she admitted. "Then I think I should feed my partner and maybe take him for a walk around the camp."

"Your partner?"

"Tracker and Latimer. Detectives for hire." She cocked one eyebrow. "What do you think?"

"I think the names should be reversed in deference to age and experience, and I think we oughta go into something a little less stressful, like maybe shark tending."

"After we solve this case, okay?"

"After we find out who went after George. Speaking of which—" She looked interested, but he chickened out. "Never mind. Pleasure before business. Let's get you unloaded."

They went back to her tent, where she first carefully stowed the eagle feathers in their pouch. He helped her with the heavy breastplate. She untied her belt and her brow band and began unwrapping her braids.

"Let me do that," he said. She let her hands drop away from the wraps and ties, and his took their place. "I've thought many times about loosening your hair. Indulge me."

"Isn't it supposed to be 'trust me'?"

"You've already said no to that." Once untied, the wraps and the ties came away easily, leaving him to comb through the ripply cascade with eager fingers. "God, it's beautiful. Why don't you ever wear it this way?"

"You sound like my kids. 'Take your hair down, Miss Tracker. Let us see how long it is.'"

"If I sound like one, it's your fault." He gathered a handful of her hair and moved it behind her shoulder. "You bring out the kid in me, Frankie. First the Ferris wheel. Now this."

"Now what?"

"Do you have a brush?"

"That's another thing my kids always want to do."

But she humored him and dug one out of her suitcase. He knew that she was humoring him, too, by standing still while he acted out a fantasy. Not the ultimate one, of course, but one that he had envisioned more than once. He would never tell her that he had thought about brushing her hair when he'd combed her favorite mare's flaxen tail, but he had. He stroked carefully, his hand following the brush. One mystery was settled. If she had been wearing jeans, her thick, shiny hair would have reached the pockets.

"Trey, those carnival tickets aren't going to last all night."

He wanted all night. He wanted to curl up with her on one of the sleeping bags that was rolled up in the corner and cover himself with the blanket of her hair. He realized how long it had been since he'd wished for such quiet intimacy with a woman. Even the wishing made him feel good.

He handed her the brush. "Let's take that walk."

"Let's get you something to eat first."

"Let's take that blanket and find a quiet place under the stars."

They compromised. The lady who had first tried to feed Trey provided them with boiled beef and more frybread, and Frankie had bottled sparkling water in her tent. It was good to leave the campground behind and climb the hill, where soft wind stirred the tall grass and cooled the late-summer night. Frankie had to lift her skirt to make the climb, but her leggings protected her calves from the crackling buckbrush.

Her hair drifted back from her face in sheets, and she felt beautiful. The long fringe swishing from her sleeves boosted her feminine ego in a way that ruffles could never have done for her. Ordinarily she would have taken Grandma's dress off and carefully stowed it away right after the dance, but it felt good to wear it now.

Above the camp and the bowery encircling the brightly costumed dancers the world felt bigger. They spread Frankie's red trade blanket in the grass and leisurely shared the food. Frankie found herself sitting in the way that was considered traditionally proper for women, with her legs tucked to one side, while Trey stretched out comfortably, set his straw hat aside and enjoyed the view.

"I wanted you to see it from here," Frankie said. "Under the lights the dancers look like colored birds, the males fanning their plumes and strutting, as males do."

"And the females, looking demure and settled, letting the guys knock themselves out to gain a little attention."

"Except you."

He chuckled humorlessly as he tore the corner off a piece of frybread. "I've been knocked out once. That was enough."

"By your wife?"

"No, I meant..." He popped the bite of bread into his mouth and thought about the response he'd given. The injury had changed his life, but it was long past time to banish it from the forefront of his mind. He'd been working on it, but maybe not hard enough. He swallowed and reached for the water bottle they were sharing. "My life seems to be divided into two chapters. Before and after I took a bullet to the head. My marriage began and ended on the 'before' side, and all that's left of that is my daughter."

"Was it one of those easily made mistakes?"

"It was her mistake, marrying a cop." He drank from the bottle, then handed it back to her with a piece of advice. "You don't ever want to marry a cop, Frankie."

"I can't imagine that your life could be limited to just two chapters. You've recovered, haven't you?"

He had no answer for that one. He sat up, draped his forearm over his knee and gestured toward the scene below. "Look at all those tents, and the campfires. And the drum really gets into your blood, doesn't it? The only thing that seems out of place is that carnival."

"It's weird, isn't it? It's for the children. The fair committee has to raise the money to bring that in. They want to provide a treat for the children, so they have fund-raisers for it. Raffles and stuff."

"The Ferris wheel was a treat for me." He dropped his head back and grinned at her. "Better than the storage room at the school."

"Why?"

"You couldn't duck away and turn the light on."

"Who'd want more lights to ruin that scene?" As she spoke, she tucked the food back into its sack. They'd both lost interest in it. "Carnivals are ugly in the daylight, but at night they're magic. They can bring out the kid in an *ex*-cop."

"That's your job," he said. "I'd forgotten what it felt like. It's been a long time."

"A long time between kisses?"

"A long time between carnival kisses." He reached up to touch her lower lip, tracing the line with one finger. "A long time between *knockout* carnival kisses."

Keep talking, she told herself. "Why? Don't they have carnivals in Denver?"

"Not like this. Not with…" He reached for her, inviting her quietly. "Come here, Frankie. Just let me hold you while we talk."

And she did, even though she knew he was making it all sound too simple. It didn't feel simple. But it did feel good. His shoulder made a wonderful pillow, and the stars were lined up above them just right, and she had about as much sense as the moon, which was melting down exactly the way her stomach was.

"Talk, then," she said stubbornly.

"Okay," he said as he shifted closer. "About how it's not like this anywhere else, right? Out here you drive along at night, miles and miles of road and fence posts, maybe a distant light here and there. Then suddenly you drive over a hill, and here's this party that nobody knows about, with colored lights and dancing and people trying to feed you."

"Haven't you been to a powwow before?"

"No. I knew about them. Sometimes I'd go to a rodeo with Luke and George, but we never took in this part of things."

"Luke was never much for Indian dancing, but George was. He got me started."

"I came looking for you tonight, Frankie. I knew you were here, and knew I wanted to see you." He turned to see her face and lifted his hand to touch her hair. "I didn't know what else I'd find. I thought I'd feel out of place, and I didn't know whether you'd want me here."

"Why wouldn't I?"

"Because I'm not part of this life, and you are. I always envied Luke, because he had so much family, and everybody helps out. Everybody's close."

She laughed, just a little. "There's no family feud like an Indian family feud, believe me." But he spoke of closeness, and she thought of his neat little house, furnished for one. "You have a family, Trey."

"I know." He sighed. "Tell you what, I haven't done very well by them. I've never really knocked myself out for anyone."

He needed touching, and in the dark she found the scar. "How did this happen?"

"Oh, it was...I got careless is all. Just one of those freak things."

"You've gone out of your way for us," she said. "Even though there's a chance—just a chance—you might not like the answers when you finally find them." The hand that had been sifting her smooth hair suddenly stilled. She could almost hear his heartbeat. His anguish became hers. She slid her hand to his cheek. "I hope it doesn't turn out to be your brother. Or your father, or anyone you care about. I hope—"

Her hope became a gratifying, openmouthed kiss. Her tongue met his, and her desire for him throbbed through her body. She pressed against him and buried her fingers in his thick, soft hair. He peppered her face with kisses, as cool as the night air, and she lifted her chin in answer to his delicious nuzzling. His hand strayed to her hip, over her bottom, then trailed along her spine.

She felt him shaking. Oh, God, she thought, but then she realized that, with his face against her neck and his hand perilously close to the dress's wide opening under her arm, he was laughing.

He drew back and smiled. "I've never tried to make love to a woman who was dressed in a suit of armor."

"Armor?" She glanced down at the heavy crust of beadwork.

"Indian armor." He moved his hand over her bottom again. "Of course, it's pretty soft here."

She responded tit for tat by clapping her hand on his hip. "And you're pretty hard in some places, Latimer, but the dress stays on."

Still laughing, he rolled to his back, taking her with him. Her fringe swished insolently. "I figured it would."

"Is this your idea of just holding me?"

"I'm holding you." Her hair curtained them while he pulled her head down and found favor with her tongue again. "And now I'm just kissing you."

"You kiss nice," she admitted. She laid her cheek against his chest, and his arms encircled her. "You always did."

"You've improved," he said. "You busy Monday morning?"

"Why?"

"I've—" A light kiss on her forehead accompanied his amendment. "*We've* got business in Aberdeen. Okay, partner?"

"Okay, partner."

Chapter 8

"Is this any way to treat a partner, Frankie?"

Frankie flinched when Trey slammed his pocket notebook on the little table by the window in the room he'd rented in the Aberdeen Homestyle Inn. One of two adjoining rooms. She had to admit, he'd been a gentleman throughout this little jaunt, up to and including the moment when she'd mentioned the fact that she was going into the construction business. Sort of.

But now he was boiling.

"When were you planning to tell me about this little scheme of yours, huh?"

She liked the way he boiled. He kept his voice down, for one thing, and his eyes flashed with sparks of fire. He stood there, hands loosely hooked low on his hips, acting as though he had the inside track on good sense. Just like a man.

Okay, maybe it hadn't been such a good idea to bring it up for the first time in the middle of their interview with Richard White at the area office. But, for her purpose, the time had been right. And White had perked up his pointy little ears and wriggled his pink rabbit nose, so she knew darn well the word was going to get out.

"It's not a scheme," she told Trey calmly, tapping her fingertips on the table. "It's…just a little ploy. Or a decoy, maybe, I don't know."

"You can't go into the construction business with Pratt. You don't know the first damn thing—"

"How do you know?" She turned her hand palm up and looked at him matter-of-factly. "How do you know I haven't been doing some carpentry on the side, huh? Summers? Teachers have summers off, you know. You have to do *something* with your summers, and I happen to be very handy with a hammer."

He jerked his head back and rolled his eyes. "I'll bet. Did Pratt buy any of this?"

"He said we could try it. He was going to talk to an attorney about whether to let me be George's proxy or something for the sake of qualifying for Indian preference on the bids, and whether that would work, or whether I'd have to become a third partner, or…" She was overdoing the explanation, and that made her uncomfortable. "I just want to hold George's options open for him until he gets better."

"Why didn't you tell me before we came down here?"

He pulled up a chair and sat knee to knee with her, which made her even more uncomfortable. No answer would satisfy him, so she offered none, even though she knew he wouldn't drop the subject. He had to talk this to death because it was in his genes. It was almost funny that white people were so predictable. This beautiful, exasperated man was going to talk this thing out as though talking might change what was already done.

"You caught me flat-footed, Frankie." He studied her for a moment. "Why did you wait until we were sitting there in front of some mealymouth bureaucrat, and then you tell *him* you're going after those housing contracts?"

"I didn't think you'd like it."

"Damn right I don't like it."

"And I knew L & M Construction wouldn't like it."

"L & M Construction," he echoed. "You still think I'm looking out for their interests? You think—" He shot out of the chair and shoved his hands into the pockets of his trim-fitting tan slacks.

Putting two paces between them, he turned to her again. "My father's business doesn't interest me, Frankie. What does interest me is that there are, according to what we found out today, four companies looking at bidding on those contracts, and only one of those companies can claim Indian preference."

"Tracker and Pratt."

"Which is still in limbo, because somebody tried to eliminate Tracker before the business even got off the ground." He shook his head, and she felt as though his eyes had pinned her to the chair. "This isn't a game, Frankie. You're not setting out decoys. You're trying to set yourself up as bait."

"Not exactly," she insisted.

"You should have discussed it with me before you—"

"Who do you think called the area office about Tracker and Pratt?" she asked rhetorically. "Hmm? Who do you think called to ask if they were still eligible for preferential status now that George Tracker was practically on his deathbed?"

"White said he didn't know."

"Do you believe that?"

"No. There may not have been any anonymous call." He sat at the foot of one of the room's two double beds. "I think White was fishing, too."

She turned forty-five degrees so she could see his face. "And I think he's fishing on behalf of your father, *Mr.* Latimer."

"Whether it's my father or somebody else, you just gave him more bait."

She chose to ignore the notion. "I *really* liked that, the way he assured you that L & M's work was held in very high regard by the Bureau. He was trying to figure out just where you stood in all this, what with your sheriff's badge and all your rather interesting connections."

"Are you—" he paused, searching her eyes for some sign "—still trying to figure out where I stand?"

"I don't know." She glanced toward the window and the bright afternoon sky. "George sacrificed a lot for this opportunity."

"I know he did."

"It stinks, and anybody with a nose on him can smell it." Resignation—the kind that felt like weakness to Frankie—crept into her voice. "Given half a chance, the Bureau will look the other way, do things the way they've always been done, because people are making money all the way down the line."

"Give me half a chance, Frankie." She felt his hand on her forearm. It was warm and comforting, and she turned to find a promise in his eyes. "Look, there are a number of variables in all this. Two other companies, for one thing."

"Two outfits that probably aren't even in the running."

"We'll see." He gave her arm a little squeeze before he drew his hand back. "The other thing is that L & M stands for more than Phillip Latimer. My father's partner submitted those preliminary bids. His signature was on them."

"So who's he?"

"I've been doing some checking on that. Dermot Messner had a construction company that did business out at Fort Belknap Reservation in northern Montana. Before that, he was part of an outfit that was based in Billings and built some houses out at Crow Agency. He knows the ropes." He raised his brow. "Now, that doesn't mean he's pulling on them illegally, but I'm betting Chuck Two Hawk can find out a lot more than I can about the man's dealings on those reservations," he said. "We'll see whether anybody was looking the other way out there."

"Two Hawk works for the Bureau," Frankie reminded him.

"Two Hawk's a cop." Since that obviously didn't hold much water with Frankie, Trey elaborated. "A lot of times people know things they can't prove. Maybe some cop out at Crow Agency knows something he couldn't prove. Or somebody up at Fort Belknap. Two Hawk will know who to call."

"So you suspect your father's partner, but not your father."

He opened his mouth for a rejoinder, then pressed his lips back together and shook his head. "What do you say we find ourselves some dinner? Maybe give this a break and just talk about old times, take in a movie. Would you like that?"

When he couldn't talk the issue quite to death, the man just turned the page. Frankie offered him no explanation for her sudden laughter and left him to assume it meant, yes, she would like that.

Rumpled and summer-time sticky, they retreated to their separate rooms. In a little while they emerged pressed and revived.

Other than her dance costumes, the slim turquoise dress was the first non-blue jeans outfit he'd seen her wear since the red blouse and black skirt. She turned the stiff collar up and left her silky hair down. She was as beautiful to him as she'd ever been—as engaging as the child, but truly heart-stirring as the woman.

And not just physically. Everything about her had him all wrought up. It sickened him that he had fallen short of her expectations. He must have, or she would have trusted him more, confided in him before she stuck her neck out with these bureaucrats and wheeler-dealers.

Too nice a neck to risk in what was stacking up to be a federal case.

Which, damn it, he wasn't going to think about for the rest of the evening.

The idea of a movie went by the wayside when dinner turned out to be a leisurely and pleasurable experience. They lingered over dessert and coffee. He offered her a cigarette, even though he'd never seen her smoke. She turned it down, but told him to go ahead. He appreciated that. He was down to one or two a day, sometimes not even that, but he enjoyed that one with the after-dinner coffee.

"Did you enjoy being a policeman?" she asked out of the clear blue.

He inhaled a lungful of smoke as he thought about

it. The word *enjoy* didn't fit, but he wasn't sure what word did.

"It was kind of like going to war, I guess. You spend a lot of hours waiting and watching, thinking you'd just like to go after somebody and get it over with, and then all hell breaks loose. It's like a flash of lightning, when everything around you is charged with deadly energy, and you're on the edge between life and death."

He tapped off some ash and watched the smoke rise and curl above the ashtray. "I used to live for the next case to break wide open. Making a bust can be a pretty powerful rush. Catching the doers of crime," he said ruefully. "It feels important. Plays hell with your family life, though."

"Considering how it played hell with your head, I imagine it was hard on your wife."

"Well, the hours are bad, and the pay isn't much better. When I was around, I wasn't really…" Frankie was listening intently, and he wanted to be honest, but he didn't want to taint the moment. He lifted one shoulder as he took up the cigarette, avoiding her eyes. "She decided I could be replaced. So, uh—" One quick drag of smoke and he managed to shrug off seven years of marriage. "So *then* we got a divorce. She wanted a different kind of a life—more social life, more people around her, more…" He offered a crooked smile. "She's a good mother, though. I can't fault her there."

Frankie was astute enough to change the subject. "Did you decide to retire early, or was the decision made for you?"

"I was injured in the line of duty. Even after they patched me up, there were problems. Different kinds of treatments, therapy, more treatments. I tried to go back on the job, but it didn't work out."

He paused, remembering the frequent migraines he'd had then, the endless succession of prescriptions, the godawful blackouts. And the fear. The fear was the worst.

"The police force and I decided to part company. They figured I was permanently disabled in some ways, and I figured..." Her face pushed back the memories, and he smiled. "I figured what I needed was some South Dakota peace and quiet and a night out once in a while with an old friend."

"Right out in public, even." She glanced furtively at the tables close by, then lowered her voice. "You don't mind it when people stare?"

"At us?" He checked out the other tables, too, and caught one guy checking back. Then he looked at Frankie again. Her eyes were chocolate sweet, and she had a mouth that would create kissing fantasies in any man's head. "I don't think they're noticing me at all."

"They're wondering what I'm doing in the Red Lion Room instead of Rocky's Bar," she said sardonically.

"You're having dinner with a man who'd love to twirl you around the dance floor at Rocky's if they don't play their music too loud." Her uncharacteristic little moue made him smile. "When we walked in here, Frankie, you turned heads."

"I know."

"You are an incredibly beautiful woman. You take my breath away." Reaching across the small table, he covered her hand with his. "When you walked into the bowery in Bullhead, you turned heads."

She smiled at him. "I'll bet you did, too."

"Yeah, I did." He chuckled. "I sure did. I almost chickened out."

"Seeee," she teased.

"Seeee," he echoed. "Okay, we are two incredibly good-looking people. If we're gonna hang out together, we're gonna attract double the attention." He shrugged as he ground his cigarette out in the ashtray. "We'll get used to it."

"We will?"

"We're partners, ain't we?"

"If you say so." She laughed. Her hair shimmied like a grass skirt when she shook her head. "I can't believe it. I used to think you were like some kind of Greek god."

"So, what was Luke? A Roman god?"

"Luke was my brother. That said it all. But you—" She leaned closer, as though she were about to share a secret, and her hair cascaded over one shoulder. "Then all of a sudden you finally noticed me, that night at the party. And you said you'd promised Luke you'd take me home."

"That was…kind of a white lie." He reached over to tuck her hair back, telling himself he was keeping it out of her coffee. It felt like corn silk. "The most dangerous kind," he added absently.

"Right," she said, smiling. "Indians know all about that, Latimer. But then…" She rested her forearm on the edge of the table and recalled, "Then you made that little joke about taking the long way home, and I thought, uh-oh, he's gonna find out I'm just *dumb*. I don't know *anything*."

"I don't know what I was thinking, Frankie." On second thought he admitted, "No, I know what I was thinking. I was thinking 'You stupid bastard, Latimer. You'd better turn this boat around and take this girl home.' But then another part of my brain kicked in."

"I won't ask you where that part's located."

The reminiscence had some teeth in it, he realized. It

gnawed at both of them. "I scared you pretty bad, didn't I? If it's any consolation, I scared myself pretty bad, too."

"I was terrified when you first put your arm around me."

He chuckled. "All the times I'd put my arm around you after we'd played basketball…"

"Without thinking about it," she said. She was watching him, and he wasn't sure what she was looking for. But he knew what she meant. "It's what you're thinking when you touch someone that makes all the difference," she said.

"And which part of your brain you're using."

"That night I knew…I couldn't be one of the guys anymore." She glanced away. "But the next time I saw you, you ignored me. And the next, and the next. So I knew I couldn't be your girl, either, because I'd acted like a child."

"Your brother would have killed me." The room felt warm all of a sudden. "I probably would have let him. You weren't much more than a child."

"I didn't tell him anything. He was sitting up when I got home that night. He took one look at me…" As did Trey, imagining that Luke had seen what he was seeing now. A rare glimpse at Frankie's vulnerability. "I tried to tell him nothing happened, but he threatened to lock me in my room until I turned eighteen."

"Wise man." Wiser than Trey, who found himself handling the memory of all this badly. "Luke is a very wise man. You were an innocent young girl, and I was as randy as a spring bull."

"I was an Indian girl," she reminded him. "And you were a Latimer. The only thing that's changed is the girl."

"Thank God." It was sincere gratitude. He wondered if God believed him. Frankie didn't seem to. "Did you know I had a hell of a time staying away from you for a while there?" She was absolutely unimpressed, but he kept trying. "Luke kept threatening to rearrange my face every time my eyes strayed. He tried to get me to enlist in the army, because he didn't think my going to college was distraction enough. I'll bet he was glad when he heard I'd quit school and left the state."

"Get out of here with this stuff, Latimer. You had girls trailing after you like…"

"Decoys," he supplied. "I remember trying to calculate how long I'd have to wait before you'd be old enough for me. Two years, you'd be sixteen, but sixteen and twenty-one was no good. Eighteen and twenty-three was getting there. At least I wouldn't get thrown in jail. I figured twenty-one and twenty-six would be pretty decent. Hell of a wait, though." He paused, looking into her eyes and wondering how far they'd come. "Is it the right time for us yet, Frankie?"

"For us?" Her brow furrowed. "This partnership of ours is on pretty shaky ground as it is, Latimer. In fact, it gets shakier all the time, what with your family and my family…"

"It'll work out a lot better if you stop going off on these crazy tangents of your own."

"It wasn't a crazy tangent. It was a good idea." She sipped cold coffee, grimaced and set the cup aside. "You just wait. Something creepy is going to come crawling out of the woodwork."

"That's what scares me, Frankie."

"It doesn't scare me." Her eyes took on a sudden sparkle. "I can't wait to just step on the thing. Just—" Her hand came down hard on the crumpled cloth napkin, rattling the cup and saucer next to it. "Squash it."

"You let me do the squashing." Damn that coy smile. "Okay? I've been known to squash a few."

The smile faded. "You won't, Trey. Not if it's—"

"We said we'd give it a break." He took her creep-squashing hand in his. "You don't know me, Frankie. I want you to get to know me."

She knew what he meant. She had known from the moment he'd suggested this trip. There were all kinds of good reasons and important purposes for coming to Aberdeen, but only one for staying overnight, no matter how many rooms they'd rented. Getting to know him was a nice way of putting it. One of his many nice ways.

The way he looked at her when they went to their rooms was another.

Big mistake on the horizon, she told herself. Gigantic, too easily made mistake. Their twin motel room doors loomed side by side, and they lingered for a moment between them. The light was dim. The hallway was quiet.

"I'm going to be knocking on the door between our rooms, Frankie. I can feel it coming."

"So can I."

With two fingers, he drew a soft line down her cheek. "If you want to pay me back for something I did or didn't do back in the old days, you can just ignore me."

"And you'll go away?"

"For the time being."

He kissed her just as softly as he had touched her, and when she turned away she had a hard time finding the doorknob. Worse, she couldn't fit her key in the lock, and she wondered what he'd drugged her with. From behind, he intruded his "expert male fingers" and slid the key into place. He pushed the door open for her. She stepped into the room and closed the door behind her without looking back.

She turned the dial on the thermostat, and the air conditioning kicked in. Quickly she undressed, wrapped her hair in a towel and climbed into the shower. A cool shower was all that was needed to temper the dry heat of the hot August night and the zinging nerves Trey had stirred up in her. Plenty of soap, plenty of lather, would take the tingling away. She made herself slippery with it, rubbing her hands over her shoulders, arms and face. The feel of her own silkiness was unexpected. Puzzling. Pleasant. She wished fleetingly for a sweeter-smelling soap.

She turned her back to the spray and lathered her belly. Her little finger brushed the scant, low-lying wellspring of hair, and she drew back as though she had scorched her finger on her own body. She slid her hands down her thighs. When he came to the door, she would be standing in the shower with the exhaust fan roaring, and she wouldn't hear him knock.

He would be well repaid.

And her needs would be ill served.

She shoved her hand through the waterfall and turned up the heat. She was no starry-eyed kid anymore, and she had to stop acting like one. Talk, talk, talk. Babble, babble, babble. Old stuff was mostly embarrassing. She didn't know why she'd kept running at the mouth. Maybe just to see what he had to say.

There were real issues to consider here, issues that had nothing to do with paybacks for ancient hurts. They had nothing to do with the fact that sitting across from him made her forget what she was eating, and sitting next to him gave her shivers and fits deep down in the pit of her stomach. They had to do with what would work and what wouldn't. Frankie used both hands to soap her face while, mentally, she drew the line in the dirt.

Lannie and George might actually work, so one of them could cross over. Didn't matter which one. You had to be a little myopic when you considered Lannie going over to George's side. And, yeah, the same went for George going over to Lannie's. But there was a lot of myopia on the reservation, and George and Lannie were too far gone on each other not to go ahead and take the leap.

Frankie and Trey would not work. Not even the worst case of blurred vision could camouflage that fact. Not even the most misdirected...

It was misdirected soap that stung her eyes. She shut the water off and grabbed another towel. Cursing the toilet for getting in her way, she rubbed and blinked, rubbed and blinked. Finally she turned to the mirror and ended up clearing the fog with her hand before she could see herself. So much for a cool shower on a hot August night.

Moments later, after she had put her nightshirt on and brushed her hair, the knock did come. She padded across the carpet and hesitated for a moment, staring at the brass knob. She hadn't used the lock. He hadn't drawn any mental lines. Obviously they were both in serious need of glasses. She opened the door.

He wore jeans and nothing else, and stood with one arm braced against the door frame. She couldn't tell whether he'd expected the door to open or whether he'd intended to open it himself if she didn't. It didn't matter. There was no longer an *if* factor.

His eyes had become blue crystal, the way she remembered them from years past, burning with an exquisite hunger for something he could not even name. But he had come seeking it anyway, and she had—maybe to their mutual surprise—just cleared the way. It was all the permission he needed. He reached for her across the threshold, and she went to him.

This time there were no soft kisses. She thought at first he would devour her when his lips claimed hers. As was her way, she stood up to him, opening her mouth to devour him right back. He groaned as their tongues plunged and parried. The kisses became quick and hard as he flexed his knees, embraced her hips and lifted her off the floor.

Lifted her. This man was *carrying* her to bed, of all things. Movie stuff. Frankie tipped her head back and laughed, delighted.

She had turned the bed down, and the sheets felt crisp and cool against the backs of her legs. He followed her down, pressing her with another supple, mint-flavored kiss. He stroked her shoulders, covered with the soft sleeveless cotton nightshirt, then drew back and smiled. The lights were low, and his shadowed smile was beautifully boyish.

"I'm glad you left the armor at home," he said as he moved his hand slowly, exploring the contours of her collarbone and the ripple of ribs below. They both remembered the heavy yoke of beads that had covered her nearly to the waist a few nights before.

"Don't lie, Latimer," she said. "You enjoy a challenge."

"I wasn't gonna break any stitches on Grandma's handmade dress." His hand slid to her breast, and he whispered, "This is much better. I can feel you through this." His fingers circled slowly, directing electrical current, charging the center pole. "God, yes, I can feel you through this."

He caressed her through the fabric until he found its hem. After that the nightshirt soon found its way to the floor. Then he took her breasts in his hands and suckled each one in its turn until she forgot her own name. He plied his mouth lower, along the shallows of her abdomen, while his thumbs flayed her nipples without mercy. Exquisite need sluiced through her, following the path of his damp kisses. She thought surely she would come apart when he took a tuft of hair between pressed lips and tugged gently, then play-bit the most tender, most sensitive, uppermost part of her thigh.

"Do you want me to go away?" he whispered. His warm breath made her shiver. Moving up again, he tickled her belly, then the underside of one breast, with his tongue. He tongued, then suckled, her nipple. "Do you?" he insisted.

"No." She answered stiffly, because she wanted to ask him to do that again. To touch her nipple with his tongue. If she said another word, it would be a plea.

He carried her hand to his body and rubbed her palm over his chest. His nipple contracted beneath the sensitive center of her hand. "Make me stay, then, Frankie," he whispered. "Undress me and keep me here all night."

He helped her with the five brass buttons that opened his jeans and liberated his manhood. He shucked his pants and sent them the way of her nightshirt, leaving them both free to touch and explore and writhe, skin to skin.

She had dreamed of this.

He had fantasized this.

She was nowhere near ready for this. It was nearly impossible to speak what she knew must be untenable for a man.

"Trey, you'll have to…" Oh, God, how should she

say it? Finish outside me? She buried her face against his neck. He had no idea how little experience she had, and she had no bravado left to carry her through. This had to be the worst… "I don't want to be pregnant," she blurted desperately. "Not without…I mean…please don't get me…"

"I won't." He stroked her hair. "Not this time, anyway." And he leaned back to show her a foil pouch he'd slipped from his pocket. "Did you think I wouldn't take care of you, Frankie?"

"No." Her face burned, along with the rest of her. "I don't know."

"Now you do." And again he stroked her, easing her back against the cool sheets. "I want to do right by you, honey. I always have." The stroking continued, down, down, over her belly and lower, until his hand cupped her mound and only his fingers stroked. "Is this right?"

"Yes, but…no, it's…"

"Yes, but no?" Two fingers dived deeper. His thumb stoked white heat in the small button of firewood she didn't even know she had stashed in her secret place. "That's even better, isn't it?"

She wanted him to stop soon, because too much was happening, and it was all happening in one place. Come inside and share it, she thought, but move quickly.

And she muttered, "I think…you should get on with the…"

"You think what?"

"Oh, Trey…" Ecstasy and panic rose together. It would be too late soon.

"Let it happen, honey."

The exhortation came from a distance. She felt as

though she were breaking apart, like the last coals of a fire. Shimmering and shuddering in a shower of red sparks.

"That's right. Let me make this happen for you."

She threw her arms around him and pressed herself against him so that he could not look at her. She was exposed to the core. His hard shaft was trapped between them now, against the hollow of her belly. He groaned and undulated, his hips moving with a liquid rhythm. She slipped her hand into the pocket their bodies made, found him, touched him. Such rigid control had to be limited somewhere along the line. She'd lost hers. There was a vacancy inside her body that urgently needed filling, and she was stroking the one and only prospective tenant. She braced her free hand against his hip and gradually levered herself upward.

"Oh, God, Frankie, not so fast. I'm not ready."

"You feel ready," she said, moving the hand that sheathed him.

"I know I feel ready." Her thumb touched a drop of liquid, and he drew a sharp breath. "Sweet heaven, do I ever."

He tore into the foil with his teeth.

"Let me help you," she whispered when he positioned the condom. He lay on his back and let her roll it down over him. Then she slid herself up farther, kissing him, touching him, reveling in the dawning knowledge that her power in this was as great as his.

"Oh, Frankie, now," he whispered as she rose above him, ready to receive him. "Come down on me. Right there."

Their joining was swift and sure.

"Oh, yes, right there," she said.

They moved together and made sensual music, unlocking the floodgates of passion and washing each other in the deluge each had dammed for the other. When all energy was spent, they slept in each other's arms.

Frankie was alone in the bed when she awoke later. The lights had been turned out. When she got her bearings, she saw that he was standing near the window, silhouetted against the sheers.

"Trey?"

"I'm just having a smoke." He raised the cigarette to his lips, then hesitated. "Does it bother you? I can do without—"

"No. I just wondered."

He took a long drag, and she watched the red ember quicken. He expelled the smoke and crushed the rest of the cigarette out in an ashtray on top of the television set. Still naked, he came back to bed and sat next to her, sliding one hand into her hair.

"Did you miss me?" he wondered.

"Yes."

He climbed in beside her and took her in his arms. "This room is like an icebox. You need me to keep you warm."

"I turned the air conditioning on full blast so I could sort of…cool off and stop thinking about you."

"Didn't work, did it?"

"No."

Making a sound of satisfaction deep in his throat, he cuddled her closer.

She breathed deeply of the masculine smell of him. Smoke. Musk. "But don't get too cocky, Latimer. It's just a crush I haven't quite managed to outgrow."

"Do you think you will?" He propped his head up on

his arm so he could see her, see her face while he toyed with her hair. "You're, what, about twenty-seven now? How much longer is this outgrowing going to take?" He made a little brush of her hair and tickled her nose with it. "Hmm? How much more time do I have?"

Smiling, she reached down between them. "*This* is what's growing, Latimer."

"Again?" He leaned back and looked down. "By damn, it sure is." She started to take her hand away, but he trapped it between them and smiled. "It wants some of that crush you're talking about." She groaned. "I can't help it, honey. You're the one who brought it up."

"Did I?" she said.

"So it's really up to you," he decided as he slid his hand over her bottom and pressed her hip against his, "to settle it back down again."

"Maybe I'll just keep it up all night."

She probably could have, if she could have stayed awake. But they wore each other out, and the only reason he wasn't sleeping at three in the morning was the dull throb centered in his right temple. It wasn't too bad. He knew if he got up and took something for it, it would subside. But it was such sweet consolation to have Frankie's head pillowed on his shoulder that he opted not to move.

She was incredible. She was everything he'd ever dreamed she would be, and more. She was both timid and fun in bed, untutored and passionate. She didn't want to trust him. That was a given. He was going to have to work to earn that precious favor, but he was willing. All he needed was a sense of what it would take.

God help him, he would find all the answers she was

looking for. He would protect her in the face of her own recklessness, no matter what the cost. He'd been telling himself he would just do a little legwork on this thing. Help Two Hawk find out for sure that Race was not involved. But the case's ties to his personal life had become the least of his worries. Now there was Frankie's safety to be considered.

He wasn't sure what she was thinking, but he was thinking he had no choice but to go the distance with this thing—and with Frankie.

Chapter 9

The following afternoon Trey was back in Chuck Two Hawk's little cubicle of an office, comparing notes. He'd dropped Frankie off at the clinic with a promise that he would be back in a little while. He'd drawn a few looks, a couple of nods, and a friendly "Hey," on his way into the police station. Maybe he was making some inroads in the trust department. Two Hawk had greeted him with a handshake, which was pretty much expected, but the smile that went with it was a bonus.

Trey laid everything he knew and most of what he suspected out on the table. He needed Two Hawk's help, and for that he had to get Two Hawk to admit that the need was mutual. One of the things he'd learned from these people was that giving was a show of respect, a way to build trust. So here it was. Every scrap of what he'd put together so far.

Two Hawk listened. When Trey was finished, Two Hawk mulled things over for a moment, then chuckled. "So Frankie's going into the construction business, huh?"

It was the one part of Trey's report that he could not be objective about, and he had to hand it to Two Hawk for exposing him right off the bat. But the policeman's eyes told Trey that he wasn't gloating. He knew Frankie, and he understood Trey's predicament.

Trey sighed. "I don't know who she thinks she's going to fool with this."

"I heard they had George out of bed yesterday and using a walker," Two Hawk said. "I thought I'd stop over later and see what else might be coming back to him."

"I'll be going over there after we finish here. I'll let you know—"

"I'd just as soon see for myself."

Understanding Trey's situation with Frankie was one thing, but the message regarding the rest of this mess was clear. There were still some conflicts. Two Hawk perused Trey's notes again, drawing a deep breath as he did so. The policeman was waiting for George to come up with a face, a name. Maybe Race Latimer. It would be simpler that way. Maybe even satisfying. But he'd read over the notes three times now, and he was making some notes of his own.

"So how do you see it, Chuck?" Trey asked. "Do you know anybody over at Crow Agency?"

"Sure. Got a brother-in-law working at the police station there. Know a couple guys up at Fort Belknap, too." He handed Trey's notebook back to him. "You know, these by-Indian contracts aren't as easy to finagle as they used to be. Used to be these white guys would pick up

some Indian off the street, put his name on their statio-
nery, and they're in business. Can't do that no more."

"But there *are* Indian businesses and by-Indian
contracts."

"Oh, sure. And there are white businessmen, maybe
like Pratt, with honest intentions. I can see where a deal
like this would work out great for George." The big
man leaned back in his chair and laced his fingers
behind his neck, adding, "But not for Frankie."

"Frankie thinks she's flushing out the bad guys,
Chuck. Trouble is, she just might."

"Then you better keep an eye on her." A grin brightened Two Hawk's stony round face. "A lot of guys
have tried keeping an eye on Frankie Tracker, but that's
about as far as anybody ever gets. She plays pretty
hard to get, that one."

"I'll worry about Frankie." Trey pocketed his
notebook. "I want to know what kind of word's out
about Dermot Messner."

"Your father's partner."

"I've never even seen the man," Trey said. "Frankly,
I make a habit of staying clear of my father's business.
I worked for him when I was a kid, and I didn't like the
idea of being groomed." He wasn't sure there was any
point in telling Two Hawk any of this, but the man *was*
listening. "Mostly I didn't like being in my father's back
pocket. But I haven't got much family, and what I've
got—" Trey shook his head "—seems to be at odds
most of the time."

"Family is family," Two Hawk said. "Race wants to
please your dad. Anybody can see that. That time I had
him in custody here…"

"You saw the way my father treats Race," Trey said.

He knew it was not to his purpose to plead Race's case right now, but the man was still listening. "Race wouldn't go that far to win the old man's favor. He'd never go that far."

Two Hawk's stony expression was at least neutral. He avoided Trey's eyes as he considered what had been said. Trey waited for a rebuttal, but he was glad when none came.

"I'll make some calls about, uh—" Two Hawk leaned forward and brought a finger down on his own yellow notepad "—this Messner. Maybe we oughta get a picture of him and show it to George."

"Maybe you could dig something like that up," Trey suggested. "While I make the man's acquaintance. A visit from his partner's son shouldn't put him on the defensive, should it?"

"Shouldn't," Two Hawk allowed. "Just keep your badge in your pocket." He followed only with his eyes as Trey stood to leave. "Why don't you get your name on the ballot, Latimer? Keep the badge in your pocket on a permanent basis." The policeman grinned slowly. "I'd probably vote for you myself."

George was looking much better. He was sitting up, a white eye patch held in place by surgical tape. From the looks of his lunch tray, he'd polished off a substantial meal. Trey took a chair next to Frankie's, and she launched into the latest news.

"One of the nurses said George had a new visitor last night. A man nobody's seen around before."

"Did you get a description?" he asked her.

"Kind of a husky redneck, sounds like. Fairly tall, about thirty years old. He was wearing a cowboy hat, which covered his hair and didn't exactly go very well with his work boots, George said."

"Who was the guy?" Trey asked George.

"He doesn't know," Frankie answered for him.

Trey laid a hand on her arm and sent a let-the-man-talk message. "Who was he, George? Maybe somebody you worked with?"

"That's what he said. We worked together." He thought about it for a moment, then shook his head. "I know I don't remember some things, but I just don't think I ever worked with that guy."

Trey knew what George was going through. Some memories returned as feelings rather than images. When there was a sense of recollection, you tried to focus it, bring it in closer. The frustration made you want to smash things.

"What did he want?" Trey asked.

"Said he was on his way back from Bismarck and missed visiting hours. Just wanted to see how I was doing." George's good eye brightened. "I'm doing good, Trey. My head's on the mend. And did they tell you I can walk? Well, my one leg is gimpy, but I'm gonna be outta here before long."

"How's the eye?"

"Looks like I might be like one of them pirates, you know? Patch, they'll be callin' me." He touched the bandage. "Gimpy ol' Gorgeous, they'll be sayin'."

Frankie laughed as she pinched the big toe that was protruding from the covers at the edge of the bed. "You think that can slow you down?"

"Lannie's going to slow him down," Trey said. "Right, George?" Smiling sheepishly, George studied a purpling IV wound on the back of his hand as Trey teased him. "I'm going to talk like Luke now. Your running days are over. I want you to be good to my sister, or else."

George smiled down at his hand. "A guy's just naturally good with a woman like Lannie."

"Listen, George…" Now, while you're relaxed, Trey thought, stir around in that haze. "Do you remember arguing with anybody the night you got hurt?"

"Lannie's—*your* brother. We got into it over Lannie."

"Got into it how? Fighting?"

"Nah, we didn't fight. He got to drinking and feeling pretty tough." George's guilelessness was as winsome as his conciliatory words. "I know how that is. We're gonna bury the hatchet, for Lannie's sake."

"I'm glad," Trey said. "You're remembering more all the time, aren't you?"

"Seem to be." George considered. "But I don't know what hit me. I swear to God—" He wagged his head, reconsidering. "The last thing I remember, I was tellin' Race off. I *really* told him off, too."

"It'll come, Gorgeous." Trey reached over to squeeze George's brawny shoulder. "You're doing great."

Frankie promised to come back soon and to bring a bag of tortilla chips next time. As he ushered her out the door, Trey wondered how far he would have to drive to find himself a plate of good tacos.

But George reclaimed his attention.

"Trey? Can you come back a minute. There's something I wanna…" He glanced at his sister. "Frankie, I need to talk to Trey."

"Same old story," Frankie complained good-naturedly. "You guys were always sending me back in the house whenever you had something *important* to talk about." Then she offered Trey a little see-you-soon wave. "I'll be out in the lobby."

"It's probably not what she thinks." George motioned Trey closer to the bed. "I wanna know how you feel about...me and Lannie."

It was a heartfelt question. Not *what do you think?* but *how do you feel?* After last night, Trey was feeling pretty good about relationships in general, and his answer came easily. "Lannie's in love for the first time in her life. I'm happy for both of you."

"Race doesn't think I'm good enough for her."

Trey shrugged. "You don't have to worry about what Race thinks, or what I think, or what anybody else but Lannie thinks."

"No, but I understand what he's thinking. I've been known to do some partying. Some cattin' around." George thumped his chest with the stronger of his hands. "Hell, I wouldn't want Frankie goin' out with a guy like me."

Because George was dead serious, Trey stifled a laugh. "How about with a guy like me?"

"You and Frankie?" George scowled. "Frankie's always saying she doesn't have time for stuff like that."

"Well, I'm trying to get her to fit me into her schedule." Trey moved back to the side of the bed, turned one of the chairs around and straddled it, smiling. "What do you think?"

"I think she could do worse. You'd treat her right, wouldn't you?"

"I'd do my damnedest," Trey promised. "How 'bout you and Lannie?"

"I don't know." Adjusting the bed covers at his waist, George stalled. Then the worries came, but softly.

Softly, so they wouldn't hurt so much. "I've been thinkin' maybe it's not fair. The doctors say I'm doin' good, but they can't tell me I won't be a cripple."

Tread lightly, Trey told himself.

"What's a cripple? People don't use that term anymore, George. Everybody's got some kind of handicap." He was repeating the easy line he'd been handed more times than he could count. He could almost accept it now.

"They can't do anything about my eye. That much is sure."

"You've still got one good one."

"And this arm doesn't wanna work right," George said, watching his left hand struggle but fail to make a fist. "This whole side. They've got me doing exercises, but…" He lifted his chin first, then his eyes. Helplessness gave way to desperation. "I can't build houses like this, Trey. I've gotta be able to work. I can't ask Lannie—"

"Give it some time." Trey cleared his throat and glanced away. He was giving the advice he'd most hated hearing, followed by the optimism that had once seemed patronizing. "Look how far you've come. You can't expect—"

"What if I can't be a husband to her? Huh? What about that? What if I can't…" George went hoarse. "What if I can't get it up?"

For a moment neither man moved.

"Have you tried?" Trey asked.

"What, here?"

"Well, you've got a door." Again he cleared his throat as he glanced at the room's second bed with its pristine, hospital-cornered sheets. "No one else is in the room with you."

They looked at each other. Under other circumstances they would have laughed. Howled, in fact, and one might have punched the other's shoulder.

Trey shook his head. "No, you're right. Give it some more time, George. Wait till the time is right, for you and Lannie. And then trust her. She's one hell of a good woman." He raised an eyebrow. "You believe that?"

"Too good for me."

"They usually are. But we muddle along, trying to mend our ways." Trey straightened his knees and pulled the chair out from the bracket his legs made. "My sister's eyes aren't sad like they used to be, George. You must be doing something right." He set the chair aside. "Keep up with the exercises. As for the other part…" A slow smile. "It's gonna come."

"Listen to you," George moaned. He shook his head, and they exchanged locker-room leers. "It's gonna *come.*"

Once he was in the hallway, Trey became a policeman again. He joined Frankie, who was visiting at the desk with Janet Silk, the shift supervisor.

"I want you to limit George Tracker's visitors to family and close friends for now," Trey instructed the nurse without preface. "You've got a pretty good idea who that would be. If the guy from last night comes back, I want to know about it."

The nurse squared her shoulders. "I wasn't on duty last night. I don't know who it was. Anyway, it's not our policy—"

"We're talking about my policy now." Trey smiled pleasantly. "Sheriff's policy."

"Well, the county sheriff doesn't usually—"

"This county sheriff does." He held up two fingers. "See, Chuck Two Hawk and I are just like this, working on this thing together, so you can be sure he'll back me up. George's visitors must be screened, and I want the names of the people who ask to see him. Descriptions, vehicles, license plates—anything you see." He jerked his thumb over his shoulder. "This desk is a ten-second walk from that window, and you can see the parking lot from there."

"I guess, if I'm on duty…"

"We'd appreciate it. You'd be helping us head off more trouble." He tapped a flat hand on the desk and gave the woman a parting nod as he steered Frankie toward the exit. "I'll check back with you, Mrs. Silk."

Once they were alone in his pickup, Trey's report was the next order of business.

"Two Hawk is making some contacts in Montana, and I'm going to ask for police protection for George."

"Do you think they might try again?" Frankie asked, worried.

"I think this mysterious visitor was interested in his condition, but I doubt if it's because he wants to see it improve." He cast her a pointed glance as he negotiated the turn onto the causeway. "I also think you ought to come stay with me for a while."

"Stay…" She made the word sound like an insult. "Stay with you? School starts next Tuesday. I have work to do. I can't just be *staying* with you."

"I'm not saying move in or anything. I'm suggesting police protection for you, too, at least until we know more about who the players are in this drama." He turned to her briefly. "And I can't very well stay with you, two doors down from the school."

"I'll be fine," she clipped.

Okay, Miss Independence… "I want to put a tap on your phone, then."

"That's a very good idea." She smiled. "An excellent idea, and it wouldn't do any good if I wasn't home."

"So, uh…school starts after Labor Day?"

"A week from today."

Don't ask. Don't even suggest.

He tried hard not to.

"Maybe we could do something together this weekend."

"United Tribes has a big Labor Day powwow at the school up in Bismarck. You'll have to bring your own tent. Do you have a tent?"

Separate tents sounded like a real thrill. "I'll get one."

The following day Trey tried to pay Dermot Messner a call, but he wasn't in his office. He tried to see Race, but he was out at a construction site. He tried not to think about the way Frankie's warm, soft skin felt against his, but he was three for three.

She called him that night.

"Trey, could you come over for a while? I think I need a little of that police protection you offered."

His response came tentatively. "Something's happened?"

"I'm scared."

If his tough little partner was scared, something had happened. He was out the door within seconds after he'd hung up his phone. Trey's pulse raced a mile a minute, trying to keep up with his pickup. If Frankie had spent the day in Wakpala as she'd planned, she should have been safe on her own home ground.

She looked shaken when she came to the door. Even as she stepped back to admit him, she tucked her chin into the open collar of the shirt that appeared gray to him. Her lower lip trembled. He closed the door, twisted the lock and turned to take her in his arms. She buried her face in the hollow of his neck and sighed.

For one prolonged moment he simply held her. Finally he asked, "You okay?"

She leaned back, looked up and smiled apologetically. "I'm being a jerk. It's no big deal. Somebody was trying to run me into the ditch on the way home from Mobridge, and if those two stupid sheriff's deputies hadn't pulled me over and frisked me earlier today, I probably would have turned around in the middle of the highway and just rammed the—"

"Hold it." He held her shoulders in his hands and took in her wild-eyed look. "Hold up a minute on the ramming and go back to the sheriff's deputies. What sheriff's deputies frisked you? I don't even have any—"

"Not yours." She shook her head quickly. "Walworth County, I think they said. The car was unmarked, but they had some kind of badges. And they had guns."

He scowled. "They held you at gunpoint?"

Yes, they held her at gunpoint.

At first she couldn't tell where the scream of the siren was coming from. The only car in her rearview mirror was a white sedan, which she'd noticed sitting behind her at the last two stoplights before she'd left Mobridge. She had taken a gravel shortcut, which was her first mistake. There was nobody else around but that white car. Then they popped out their portable red flasher, and she groaned as she pulled over to the side of the road. She hadn't been speeding, so it had to be one of those petty deals off-reservation police liked to stop Indians for, like her license plate was dirty or something.

"Get out of the car, and keep your hands high."

She looked in her rearview mirror again. She saw two open car doors, two cowboy hats and two pistols trained over the tops of the doors right at the back of her head.

"Don't make any sudden moves."

Was he serious? This didn't happen in real life. The absurd instructions were shouted through a bullhorn. Frankie gauged the distance between her and the nearest farmhouse, which was maybe half a mile off the road, and wondered if anyone there could hear the voice. If they could, what were they doing? Calling the whole family over to the window?

"Move!"

He actually sounded serious. Theatrical, but serious.

She pushed the door open and let her boots drop to the gravel. She got out slowly. Then she remembered her hands. She felt silly putting her hands up as though she were playing cowboys and Indians, but she did it. She even turned to see whether they were satisfied that she was doing it right.

"Don't turn around. Put both hands on the top of the car door."

She gripped the door and stared straight ahead. This was fast becoming very unfunny. When she heard footsteps crunching up behind her, she turned her chin to her shoulder. "What's this all about? Did I make an illegal turn or something?" She was trying to sound huffy. She hoped she was pulling it off.

"If you speak English, you must be able to understand it, lady. I said do not—" he jerked on her tidy French braid, forcing her face forward "—turn around."

"Who are you?" she demanded through clenched teeth.

"Sheriff's deputies." He flashed a badge over her

shoulder, and along with that she glimpsed the steel barrel of his gun. "Walworth County."

She heard the approach of a second man. "What's she carrying? Anything?"

"I don't know yet." The first man put his foot between hers and tapped her right boot. "Spread 'em."

"Wha-what?"

"Spread your legs. You know how to do that, don't you?"

Oh, God, the creep was going to do something horrible to her. "P-please, I haven't done anything."

"Just routine, lady. Don't make any sudden moves."

She couldn't have hidden much in her summer shirt and jeans, but he searched. Up one leg, down the other. She tried to put her mind somewhere else, but the hands that felt her body everywhere, *everywhere,* were those of a man who knew what he was looking for. And he was finding it.

It took forever. Frankie's stomach rolled, and she thought she would vomit before he was through. When he finally backed away, only the top of the car door, which was cutting into her palms, kept her from falling forward.

"Where's your ID?"

She lifted one hand. "My purse is on the floor."

The contents of her purse were scattered in the gravel. She risked a peek. Billfold, hairbrush, the beaded tassel with the key ring that held her school keys. Oh, Lord, a tampon rolled over the gravel, and the wind pushed it against the toe of the man's brown work boot. He kicked it away as he rifled through her billfold.

She had to stop cowering, she told herself. She had to face them. These guys were supposed to be lawmen, and she was a law-abiding citizen.

"What are you looking for?" she demanded. "You have no right—"

"Identification."

"Why don't you ask? You can't just do this to people."

"We can if the individual poses a threat. We have reason to believe you're armed."

"Armed with what? You've got the wrong *individual,* mister." She turned, fists clenched at her sides. They both wore mirrored sunglasses. The short one used his free hand to shade a spot on her back window to permit him to peer in. "Do you have a search warrant? You can't search my car without—"

"She's right," the taller one said. "We can't search the car without a warrant."

"I know my rights," Frankie insisted. "Which, by the way, you haven't read me."

The taller one was chewing gum and grinning. "She's right again."

"And I want to see my—" Her mouth was dry. She clenched her jaw and snapped her eyes from one ugly face to the other. "You know, my boyfriend is the sheriff of Corson County. He's not going to like this."

"Well, see, we don't have to read anything to you unless we arrest you." The tall creep handed her the billfold. Her Social Security card fluttered to the ground. "This is your lucky day, Frances. You are not under arrest."

Short Creep chimed in, "Next time, sweet cheeks. Next time we'll have a warrant that'll get us right down into your underwear."

Her face flamed and her throat burned as she watched them walk away, but she didn't cry. She felt as though her skin was covered with maggots, but she would not cry.

"So how was she?" she heard Short Creep ask.

"Hey, that little squaw is built like…"

Trey sat next to her on the sofa and listened to the story. She left out some parts, trying to get through it quickly. He said nothing, just listened. His eyes were glittering with anger by the time she finished, but he simply took her hands in his, which were blessedly gentle, wonderfully steady. Hers were shaking again.

"And the car that tried to run you off the road?"

"It was a different car. Black or…some dark color. It kept speeding up and bumping me from behind. Had his brights on. Just about blinded me." She bit her lip, recalling her own efforts to beat back panic and keep her car on the road. "Pretty soon he passed me and barreled on down the highway."

"The deputies." Trey paused. "There were two of them?"

"Yes."

"Did you see much of the badge?"

"I'm pretty sure it said Walworth. I saw a *W*."

He nodded. "We're going to call Jim Heck. He's the sheriff over there. I don't know the man very well, but if these guys are his deputies, they're in for some trouble. They violated every standard in the book, even if it was mistaken identity."

"What do you mean *if?*" Frankie retorted. "I didn't even run a red light."

"You're being harassed."

"Obviously." Then she realized what direction his reasoning was taking, and she shook her head. "Trey, this has nothing to do with George. They had the badges and the guns, and they were—" She hated the way her voice was rising. She took a deep breath and expelled the word. "—cops. Cops are supposed to protect people from being…violated like that."

"Frankie, you…"

Trey caught himself. It didn't matter that she'd gotten herself into this. He was going to have to get her out of it somehow.

"You can't trust anybody these days," Frankie muttered.

"Can you trust me?" His heart ached when she turned her face away from him. Her eyes glistened as she pressed her lips together tightly. Her profile was the image of bravery on the verge of collapse. Silently he invited her to let go, to use him for support. "I need to know that you trust me, Frankie. If you'll just…"

"Hold me, please."

He opened his arms, and she curled herself into his embrace. "Oh, Trey, it was horrible," she whispered. "They had guns. They pointed guns right at my head."

He closed his eyes and ran his hands up and down her back. "I have guns, too. Do you know how to use one?"

"I've shot a .22 rifle before." She hated crying. She wiped her eyes with her hand and worked to find a cheerier note. "You know what I told them? I told them my boyfriend was a sheriff, too, and he wasn't going to like this one bit."

"He doesn't." Trey leaned back. He smiled wistfully as he brushed his thumb over her damp cheek. "Am I your boyfriend now?"

"It sounds kind of silly, doesn't it?" She gave a breathy little laugh. "My boyfriend. Why didn't I say 'my partner'?"

"Either way, I'm making progress. You threatened them with me instead of your big brother."

She laid her head on his shoulder, and they sat holding one another quietly. He made a mental list of the steps he would take to find out what in hell was going on here. He hadn't figured on the neighboring county sheriff's office being a party to all this. He hadn't appointed any deputies since he'd taken the job. Hadn't needed any. Too often, the supposed power went to people's heads. He stroked Frankie's arm and absently wondered whether her sleeve was green or pink. He was guessing green.

"Have you ever had to frisk a woman, Trey?" she asked in an unusually small voice.

"Yeah." He rested his chin against her hair. "It goes against the grain, but it's necessary sometimes."

"Do you have to…" She hesitated, and felt her shoulders stiffen. "Are you supposed to touch them that way?"

"What way?" he asked guardedly.

"You know." Her voice quivered. "In intimate places. What could I have hidden between my breasts or between my…"

"No!" He bit back a vicious curse and fought for control. He didn't want to scare her or to make her feel any worse. Protectively, he pulled her closer, stroking her hair. He spoke quietly. "Did they hurt you?"

"They made me feel…kind of dirty."

He closed his eyes, and a red mist filled his head. Bright, blood red, the only red hue he was capable of distinguishing. Again he spoke quietly. "They had no right to do that to you, Frankie."

"But I'm an Indian, Trey. Some people think—"

"Some people are gutter scum. They shouldn't be in the same world with you, honey, but they are."

"When they were walking away, one of them said I,

um…" There was a catch in her breath. "Ha-had a nice set of, um…"

"Oh, jeez." With his hand against her hair, he pressed her head against his chest. He would have given anything to have been able to absorb her into himself and to become her armor. "I'll find them for you, Frankie. I promise you, I will." He looked into her wide, frightened but, yes, trusting eyes. "I'm not leaving you alone tonight. I want to take you to my place. Nobody will bother you there."

"Okay," she said with a wisp of a smile. "But just for tonight. I'm used to standing on my own two feet, you know."

"That was before you got yourself a partner."

Chapter 10

A steady rainfall cooled the early-morning air. Trey's bedroom windows were open, and he was surrounded by the pelting sound, the fresh water-and-clay smell and the gray mantle of a rare Dakota rain. It made the early daylight hours an especially good time for dozing in the arms of a warm, well-loved woman.

He'd always been a light sleeper, needing only a few hours. But since the shooting, those few hours came in the early morning. He'd begun calling himself a night owl, although not for love of darkness, which he found oppressive. He hated waking up in the dark and feeling, however fleetingly, that he was back in the tunnel. Daylight and pattering rain and the warmth of Frankie's breath on his skin reassured him.

He would gladly have stayed in bed all day. The cool, damp air on his face made the parts of him that were snuggled beneath the cotton sheet and blanket feel all that much cozier. He would have enjoyed the cycle of drifting to sleep and awakening to the sight of her sleeping face several times more. But he had to feed a couple of horses and see a man about a couple of jack-asses he'd apparently deputized.

Frankie stirred against him deliciously.

"Good morning, Miss Frances," he said as he brushed his lips and nose over her luxuriant black hair. "In a few days they'll ring those Ding Dong School bells, and you'll be taking roll call."

"Mmm, but not today."

"No. Today I'm the one who has to get to work."

"Mmm, but not this early." She shifted to her hip and stretched her arm around his chest.

What heavenly bonds, he thought. "You could make a man miss his own roll call. Even the one up yonder."

She pressed several kisses near his nipple before she set her chin next to it, looked up and smiled lazily. "And who would they be calling? Is Trey Latimer the whole, entire name they have written for you in that big atten-dance book in the sky?"

"Not exactly. Trey means three, right? I'm the third Phillip Latimer. You would have known that if you'd ever been in a class with me. First roll call, I'd always set the teacher straight." He shoved his arm behind his head and gave a pseudomeaningful look and the usual fair warning. "Don't ever call me Phillip."

"Can't I call you Phillip, even sometimes?"

"With a smile like that, you can call me anything you want anytime." He touched the corner of her smile with one finger. "Just call me. Like you did last night."

"I like Trey better. I don't know any other Treys. Lots of Phillips, but only one Trey."

"There won't ever be a Phillip Latimer IV, that I can promise you."

"No sons?"

"I'd love to have a son." He wondered whether it was too soon to ask her, in a solemn and masterful tone, to bear him one. The corners of his mouth twitched at the thought of the incredulous look she would probably give him. "But there's something about hanging your name on your kid that kind of says you've got plans for him to be just like you. And if that doesn't turn out, there'll be hell to pay."

"What kind of hell?"

"Oh, just…bad blood. My father never approved of my interests or my plans or my friends. None of it interested him." But from her attentive eyes he could tell how much it interested Frankie, which prompted him to tell her more. "As for me, I guess I didn't much care for the way he treated people. Especially my mother."

"I don't remember her. Was she like Lannie?"

"Lannie's turning out to be a lot stronger."

"I like her. I'm sure I would have liked your mother."

Ah, Frankie, he thought as he pushed her night-tossed hair back from her beautifully sculpted cheek. She should have had the chance to meet you.

"My mother was sick a lot. Most of the time my father acted like he didn't know he had a wife. And then Race came along, and suddenly we had this little brother. I was grateful for the brother, but not for all the hard feelings that came along with him."

As always, his apology for his own share of the hard feelings followed quickly.

"Race was just a little kid, you know? None of it was his fault. My dad treated him the same way he treated my mother. Like he wasn't even there. He was my father's responsibility, and my father took care of his responsibilities. But Race wanted to be his *son.*"

She was still listening, but she had laid her cheek against his chest when he spoke of hard feelings. Her fingers stirred soothingly over his belly, encouraging him to talk about whatever he would have her hear.

"One time, when he was maybe about Tricia's age, he shined six pairs of the old man's boots. Lined them all up in front of the closet door and waited for him to come into his room and find them. And I mean, every pair was gleaming. Sergeant Luke Tracker himself couldn't have done better." At that, she lifted her head and smiled, but the memory killed his will to smile back. "So the old man comes in, wants to know who dragged all his boots out of the closet. Race just stood there, waiting for some kind of…" He shook his head. "Some kind of love, Frankie. Just some kind of sign."

"Did your father thank him at least?"

"Yeah, with a swat on the butt. Told him to put everything back in the closet and stay away from his personal stuff. Damn, I just wanted to shake that man and tell him to get his fat head out of his—" Her eyes widened expectantly, and he pushed himself up, reaching back to plump a pillow into place for support. "'Course, I was about half his size."

Frankie grabbed the bed sheet when Trey's movement shifted everything and adjusted it modestly over her breasts. "Did you talk to Race?"

"I tried. He ran out of the house. Two hours later I found him hiding in a culvert. He was a tough little guy, and he kept it all inside. I wasn't as good with him as Lannie was. She pretty much raised him."

"Then I don't see how he turned out so—" She lifted one shoulder. "Well, he's not like you."

Trey spread his arms, inviting her to make him her pillow, and she did. He tucked her head beneath his chin. "What am I like?" he wondered.

"You don't act like you're better than everybody else. Neither does Lannie."

Trey chuckled. "I've been gone a long time, honey. It's easy for me to come back smelling like a rose."

She nuzzled the golden hair on his chest. "I don't know about roses, but I know what a snob smells like. I'm sorry, but that brother of yours, the way he acted about George…"

"Race has a chip on his shoulder, granted. And George has himself quite a reputation to live down." He drew his head back for a look at her winsome face. "Granted?"

"He's changed."

"I don't really know what he was like before. I just know that my sister loves him the way he is now. And I know that Race is going along with my father, and that one of these days he's going to realize that it's not getting him anywhere."

"I wouldn't want any sister of mine going out with that brother of yours, I can tell you that."

"Why? Because he's part Chippewa?"

"He acts like a Chippewa. Meaner'n—yow!"

A playful pinch on her hip had her squirming sweetly. He growled and reversed their positions, tucking her underneath him. "Do we have to have all the Trackers and the Latimers in this bed with us? Do you realize how crowded it's getting?"

"Kick 'em all out, then," she suggested as she slid her arms around him. "It'll just be us."

He kissed her lips, then her cheek, then her morning-soft eyelid. Dewdrop kisses, meant to tell her how glorious it was to start the day with her. Then he rolled to his back, taking her with him. They held each other chest to chest so that neither could see the other's smile. But each felt the other's joy. Their heartbeats combined, and it was wonderful just to lie there and let it happen.

"You didn't sleep much last night," she said.

"I have trouble with that sometimes." He pressed his cheek against her hair and closed his eyes. "But I slept better than usual. You're nice to sleep with."

"You too." She paused, and he felt the muscles in her shoulder tighten. "I had a dream about being in the car out in the middle of a field. It was weird. The car wouldn't start, and I knew something was lying in the field up ahead. Something that didn't want me there."

He'd learned to respect bad dreams. "What did you do?" he prompted.

"Nothing. I just sat there, waiting. I woke up, and you were here." She dropped a kiss high on his chest before she drew back, taking the sheet with her as she sat up. "Not that I'm going to be a big baby about all this, but I was glad you were here."

He tucked his arm behind his head and smiled, feeling content. He'd kissed and caressed every part of her, but still she took the sheet. She swung her hair back and forth as though shaking out the night's wrinkles. It brushed the dimples on her bottom.

He swung his legs over the side of the bed and plucked his jeans off the floor. "What do you want for breakfast?"

"How about Froot Loops with bananas?"

"How about oatmeal with raisins?"

"How about toast and coffee?"

"I can manage that." He turned, seeking her across the wide white plane of the bed they'd shared. She'd slipped into a white shirt of his, but she was watching his buttoning process rather than her own. Maybe his hands slowed a fraction on the last two, but at least he'd lined the buttons up with the right holes, which was more than she could say.

He thought of making a flying tackle across the bed. He actually saw himself in flight.

"What are you grinning about, Latimer?"

"You missed a button," he said as he made himself head for the kitchen.

They padded across the cool floor on bare feet. He did the coffee, she the toast. She told him he ought to buy Froot Loops, and he promised to stock up.

"Listen," he began, broaching a serious subject with a serious tone. "I called Jim Heck last night, and it sounds like those two bastards might actually be his deputies."

"And you're disappointed." She leaned her hip against the counter and watched him add sugar to his coffee. He spared her a puzzled glance. "You thought they were the guys you've been looking for, and that they were just pretending to be sheriff's deputies," she supposed.

Close enough. "You read me like a book, Watson."

"Well, you had it right the first time, Latimer. I was being harassed." She nodded when he switched the spoon to the other cup. "And if I put up a fight, it's my word against theirs. Two against one."

"You won't be putting up any fight without me." He stirred, then handed her the richly scented brew.

"You weren't there when it happened," she pointed out before sampling a sip. "So it's still two white lawmen against one Indian woman. The odds aren't good."

"You're not just going to let it go, are you?"

"No. I'll fill out their papers." She stared out the window. The sound of rain splattering on the front step filled the seconds she allowed for reflection. "I don't want to see those men."

"I know." He, too, watched the water slide down the glass. "But *I* do."

Trey took Frankie to the neighboring county courthouse and introduced her to Jim Heck, the sheriff. He was tall and shapeless but for the potbelly that resembled a cherry sucked into a soda straw. He had the limp personality to match.

Frankie squared her shoulders and took a deep breath. "I want to file a complaint against two of your deputies for…for what they did to me yesterday."

"Jenkins and Stoller." Heck's head bobbed in what seemed more like a nervous tic than a sign of assent. "It's like I told Trey when he called, I thought they might have been my boys. They were in this morning—I called them in myself. And they said they pulled you over," he admitted.

"They didn't tell me their names."

"Well, you were probably a little nervous." He dropped his flat butt into his desk chair and rolled out the top right-hand drawer. "They filled out a report. I have it right here." It was two pages. The shadow of handwritten lines showed through the translucent paper. "Says they identified themselves. Unfortunately, your car matched the description of one driven by an individual who was seen shooting at road signs within the city limits."

"They never told me why I was stopped," Frankie said flatly.

"Well, that's what it was." Heck eyed her pointedly over the tops of the papers. "And this was off the rez."

"Is that supposed to mean something?" Trey challenged.

"It means this is our jurisdiction, and we take every report seriously."

"How about my report, sheriff?" Frankie asked calmly. "Will you take that seriously?"

"They stopped the wrong car. It happens. According to their statements, and they both tell the same story here—" he raised one paper, then the other "—they wasted a few minutes of your time, maybe shook you up a little, but sometimes that can't be helped."

"Can't be—"

Trey's gut was beginning to twist, but he laid a hand on Frankie's shoulder and betrayed nothing of himself to this man. "Frankie's ready to put her statement in writing, too. Do you have a place where she can sit down and do that?"

"Sure." Heck handed her a form with a staple in the corner. "Here's what we'll need. Just tell it in your own words, the best way you can...."

"I'm a teacher, Sheriff. I know how to read and write."

Heck stepped around his desk and pointed across the hall. "You can use the clerk's desk there."

Frankie glared at the man, but he avoided her eyes as he ushered her out and closed the door.

Trey lit a cigarette. "What kind of a report were they investigating?" he asked, peering at the man through a dissipating cloud of smoke.

"Telephone tip."

"Anonymous?"

Heck squatted and rolled his chair under his pre-seated shape. "I don't know how it was logged. It came into the police station."

"Did they have a license plate number? Any description of the suspect?"

"Look, these guys are part-time." He looked up and made a squinty face, while Trey made more smoke. "You know how that is. They stopped the wrong car. Just one of those things."

"One of what things? You don't draw weapons on the basis of an anonymous phone tip."

Heck smiled indulgently and shrugged, as if to say, "What can you do with these kids?" Trey wanted to offer a couple of graphic suggestions, but he restrained himself.

Instead he pushed some papers aside and braced his hands on the edge of Heck's desk, hovering over him like an avenging angel. "So how stupid are Jenkins and Stoller? Do they know the difference between a pat search and a cheap feel?"

Heck's eyes bugged, and his voice went up an octave. "They didn't say anything about an improper search."

Trey's laughter was caustic.

Heck fidgeted, fingering the edges of the papers containing his deputies' stories. "I won't tolerate any horsing around. I'll be sure and ask them just how they conducted themselves."

"You do that. Tell them they'd better get their story straight for the state's attorney, too."

"Are you making this a personal thing, Latimer?"

"Your deputies made it a personal thing."

Trey straightened, but he kept the man under his

close scrutiny as he carried his cigarette back to his mouth and drew deeply. His head was beginning to throb, and he knew he was doing himself a disservice. But he didn't mind adding anything he could to Heck's discomfort.

"Damn, if she can claim some kind of sexual thing, I'll have every women's group in the county down on my neck." Heck glanced away and patted the desktop with a flat hand.

He looked up at Trey again. "I don't get it. Now, you're Phillip Latimer's son, right?" Trey nodded once. "I've got that right. And I was under the impression—correct me if I'm wrong—that there was some bad blood between the Trackers and L & M Construction. One of the Trackers horning in on you guys' contracts."

Here it comes. Talk to me, Heck, baby.

"Who told you this?" Trey asked calmly.

"Your dad's partner. I've been playing golf with Dermot this summer." As if he thought that bought him a ticket to something, Heck smiled tentatively. "You know, he's brought a lot of business to this town. He bought the sand and gravel outfit south of here, got that back on its feet. He gets a lot of government contracts, which is good for the town. Great for you guys."

"That it is," Trey agreed, maintaining a poker face. "Do Jenkins and Stoller work for L & M, by any chance? I've kinda lost track of Dad's employees."

"Vern Stoller does. And Tommy Jenkins drives truck for Messner Sand and Gravel."

"Well, that's interesting." He wondered which was the tall one Frankie had told him about. The one whose teeth were already history.

The door opened, and Frankie came in with her

papers. Trey extinguished his cigarette in what he assumed was an ashtray and announced, for her benefit as much as Heck's, "We're going to ask for a restraining order on your part-time deputies."

"You a lawyer now? I thought you were a cop."

"I thought I was a retired cop, but I'm picking up new titles every day." He turned to Frankie and gave her a subtle wink. "Right, partner?"

Frankie couldn't help smiling. "That's right."

After Trey took Frankie home, he paid a visit to L & M Construction. He found himself walking in on an apparently chilly confrontation between Phillip and Race over a set of blueprints. Trey recognized all the signs of an idea shot down. Race was consoling himself with a cigarette, while Phillip rolled up the plans and snapped a thick rubber band on them, a sound that sang out, "My way."

"You need a job?" Phillip demanded. It was the closest thing to a greeting he was likely to offer. "Put you on with your brother. Maybe you can get this project moving. Simple, straightforward retaining wall. That's all it is."

"It's in the wrong place." Race's tone indicated he was not saying this for the first time. He was sitting in the corner of the room on a two-drawer filing cabinet. "It'll look like a jigsaw puzzle in two years."

"I pay soil experts for that kind of information. You're no expert, so don't try to tell me what I'm paying experts to tell me." Phillip tossed the rolled-up blueprints on his desk and sighed. "What's the good word, Trey? You getting out of the horse business?"

"Nope. The horse business—" he and Race exchanged *simpatico* glances "—is still *my* business. Even though I'm no expert, I'm enjoying it." Trey helped himself to a chair. "I still have a hand in the law enforcement business, though, and I've been trying to meet this elusive partner of yours. I've got a few questions I want to ask him."

"Messner? If you hang around a while, you might catch him," Phillip said. "He's putting together a deal in McLaughlin."

"Indian housing?" Trey asked.

The ash fell from Race's cigarette, landing on the carpet. Race dropped his boot heel into the nap and twisted it a couple of times.

"Well, most of that's on hold right now." Phillip reached across the desk for his souvenir casino ashtray and tossed it to Race, who made the catch with an economy of motion. Then, to Trey, he added, "As you probably know."

"I know there's a question of Indian preference."

"The government can pass over the Indian bid if they don't think the company can handle the job."

Or if the Indian partner is taken out of the picture.

Trey studied the pickup keys he still held in his hand and put his next question almost indifferently. "Do you have somebody looking out for you in the Bureau?"

Phillip pushed his chair back from his desk and folded his arms. "I wouldn't say looking out for us exactly, but you try to get to know people who can do you some good."

"Is that what you did?" Trey wondered as he ran his thumbnail over the long groove in one of the keys. "Do you make it worth their while to do you some good?"

"That's how business is done. Messner calls it 'fieldwork.' This by-Indian policy gives them an edge, so we've got to counter that with a little wining and dining. Nothing wrong with that."

Trey looked at Race, whose expression was unreadable. He turned to his father and asked quietly, "What would be wrong with making your Indian son a full partner?"

Phillip's chortle ended in a snort, with his arms bouncing on his chest. "Why? To get in on the preferential treatment they get? I don't believe in it. Race knows what I think of all these minority shenanigans. The sooner we all—"

"The sooner we all jump into the melting pot, the better off we'll be," Race finished for him. He slid off the filing cabinet as he took a last drag on his cigarette, blew a long, lazy stream of smoke and jammed the butt into the glass dish. He eyed his father. "What if I'd been born to the same mother as Trey?"

"What do you mean?"

"I've been working for you for almost five years," Race said quietly.

"You've got a good job. You're a crew foreman. That's about all the responsibility you've earned."

Race's eyes were smoldering. Phillip dismissed both the man and the issue by turning away.

But Trey saw a flash of the boy and the row of boots and the glittering black eyes. "What's with you, Dad?" he asked. "Your main thrill in life is keeping people under your thumb. Nobody can live *with* you. Everybody has to be *under* you."

Phillip leaned across the desk and wagged a finger at his older son. "You made your big break, and where did it get you? I offered you a piece of this business, but you threw it back in my face. You've never appreciated what I could give you."

He swiveled his chair toward Race, again pointing his finger. "And *you*. Race, you have no ambition, no real sense of responsibility. You want to go out and raise hell every weekend, just like your mother. And Lannie's such a homely old maid, she's throwing herself at some Indian bum. I had to go outside this family to find myself a partner who could help me make this business grow."

Trey felt sick as he watched his brother stride toward the desk. He didn't know if he had the heart to stop Race from shutting the old man's mouth for him.

Race took off his black-and-white cap and contemplated the L & M logo on the crown as he plowed his hand through his flattened hair. He glanced at Trey before he tossed the cap on Phillip's desk, followed by a clattering ring of keys.

"What do you think you're doing?"

It was one of their father's favorite questions, calculated to elicit a heated retort. Trey still hated the sound of it, still wanted to spit out the first foul answer that came to mind. He saw a muscle twitch in Race's jaw.

"What I should have done a long time ago," Race bit out. He was still looking at the cap. "The tools in my pickup belong to me. I've got some pay coming. Give that to Lannie. I want her to have a nice wedding, no matter who she marries."

He lifted his head and stared at his father. Rage and pain warred with one another in his dark eyes. "I never had a chance with you, did I? Not from the day my lazy, irresponsible mother, whoever she was, dumped me in your lap." He shook his head, and his voice nearly broke. "I've already hung around you too damn long."

Race walked out, slamming the door behind him.

"You had three chances," Trey told his father quietly. "I think you just struck out."

It had stopped raining. Race was leaning against Trey's pickup, waiting, another cigarette in his hand. He held it out as an offering, and Trey accepted. The acrid smoke pinched his lungs, but it was something to be shared.

Trey handed the cigarette back. "Where are you headed?"

"I don't know." Race studied the reinforced toes of his work boots. "I'm not running away. I'm just getting the hell out."

"I know."

"Yeah, you know." Race lifted his chin and sent another gray cloud toward the gray sky. "Are you still trying to find out what happened to George Tracker?" Only after he'd voiced the question did he look over to see Trey's nod. "Listen, there's a couple of guys that Messner hired who don't seem to have too much to do except drive around. One's Vern Stoller, and the other one's name is Sheldon Tate. Tate's from Montana. Big cowboy."

"And Stoller is a sheriff's deputy in his spare time."

"Yeah. Kind of a little jerk who likes to flash that stupid badge around and talk about the kind of guns he likes to use." Race shook his head. "I doubt if he's ever fired a shot. But I'd bet Tate has. Both of these guys have plenty of spare time, but they're on the payroll. Messner made a comment recently, kind of a joke, about Indian competition being easy to eliminate. He wants those government contracts."

"How does our old man fit into all this?"

"He doesn't ask Messner about his *fieldwork*. Start-ups are slow, and the company needs the business," Race said. He glanced toward the office building, and Trey wondered whether Race was hoping the front door would open. They both knew it wasn't going to. "Phillip Latimer's the same workhorse he's always been," Race concluded bitterly. "Nobody can do the job as well as he can."

He pitched his cigarette into a puddle and offered Trey a handshake. "Listen, you take it easy."

Trey gripped his brother's hand. He looked vulnerable somehow, like the kid whose hat had been stolen by the school bully. Trey took off his straw cowboy hat and stuck it on Race's head. Race adjusted the brim and looked to Trey for approval.

"Much better," Trey told him. "You're welcome to stay at my place."

"Thanks, but I think I'm due for a change of scenery." Suddenly the infectious grin was there, and there was a small spark in Race's eye as he punched Trey's shoulder. "But I'll be watching the newspapers to see if you get your man."

Trey watched his brother's pickup turn south. His mind was bombarded by all the things he should have said. All the things he should have done differently. Damn. He had no right to try to stop him.

But he had a right to his regrets. Every useless one of them.

He might have punished himself by spending the evening alone if he hadn't been worried about Frankie. He had a pretty good idea what he was up against now, and he had to protect her while he found a way to prove what he knew.

Frankie's half of the little duplex set aside for

teachers was two doors away from the school. Trey parked his pickup next to her car, figuring police protection was the best reason in the world for him to be there. And the world could accept it or shove it.

Police protection was also a good reason to carry a gun, and Trey took his automatic pistol from the glove compartment, along with a box of shells. She needed protection, he told himself as he turned the weapon over in his hands. Serious protection, offered by a man who wouldn't break out in a cold sweat at the thought of a gun pointed at his head. What he had to think about was those two guns that had been pointed at *her* head. And then he had to remember to use it.

Use your head, Latimer. Don't lose it.

And if it starts lightning, get that tin head of yours inside.

Trey smiled, silently wishing his brother luck. He strapped his pistol around his waist before he went to the door.

She was glad to see him, and that made him feel good. He decided to put off all potentially unpleasant discussions. When he caught her eyeing the pistol, he quietly took it off and set it aside, thinking he would try to be discreet about keeping it close by. He hadn't told her what he knew about Stoller and Jenkins yet. He wanted to talk to Chuck Two Hawk First. He needed to know how Messner's Montana operation had worked. Then he would need a little help from George.

And he needed to be with Frankie tonight. He wanted to unbraid her hair and bury his face in it.

"How about a great Denver omelet at my place?" he

offered as he rubbed his hands up and down her arms and gazed into her eyes.

"How about some soup and frybread over here?"

"We've done this number before. I bought Froot Loops today."

"And I made frybread." She put her arms around his neck and kissed him sweetly.

He smiled wearily. "I'll eat whatever you put on the table. How's that?"

"Does that mean I win?"

He nodded. "But let's go to my place later. Otherwise, who's gonna eat all those Froot Loops?"

They shared a quiet supper and later stood hip to hip at the sink doing dishes. Trey felt that he was home by her side. The place didn't matter, although there were nice touches of her clean-line taste in the southwestern decor. He wondered what her shades of gray really were. Experience told him they were red hues, not green. Those were the colors he had trouble distinguishing, filling his world with more than the usual shades of gray. Whatever her colors, he felt comfortable with them. He stacked the last pot in the dish drainer.

"Race is gone," he said without preface.

"Gone?"

He nodded as he dried his hands on the towel. "The old man kicked him in the gut once too often."

"Then I guess it's time he left." She used the other end of the towel for her own hands.

"Unless he's the one who assaulted George?"

She took the towel from him, set it aside and put her hands at his sides, over his belt. She looked into his eyes to tell him, "I don't believe that anymore."

"Why?"

"Because if he was, you wouldn't have let him go." She laid her face against his shoulder and whispered, "I don't feel like driving anywhere. Do you?"

He put his arms around her and rubbed her back. That braid begged to be dismantled. He slid the covered elastic band off the end and let his fingers go at it.

"That red pickup of mine is hard to miss," he warned.

"I know."

"I need you tonight. I need to be with you."

"I know that, too."

She took him to her bedroom, filled with plump pillows and books and pictures of children and horses. He laid his pistol on the night table next to a framed photograph. He paused, reached for the picture and recognized his own adolescent likeness. Had he really looked that young and innocent?

"I confess to being a Trey Latimer groupie," she said, laughing as she turned the lamp down low.

"I wish I'd known. I'd have been back sooner."

She knew he needed extra coddling tonight, and she vowed to give him that. He kissed her slowly, softly, again and again, while she unbuttoned his shirt and unbuckled his belt. She caressed his chest, smiled and whispered, "Prickly," before she touched her lips to his soft curls. His throaty chuckle deepened when she caressed his belly and eased his zipper down, slipping teasing fingers beneath the elastic of his shorts.

"Oh, jeez, Frankie, that's not fair."

"Even it up, then," she challenged as she sheathed him in her hand and stroked him gently. "But you must start at the top," she warned.

Her top was gone quickly. He filled his hands, then

his mouth, with her breasts and eased her back against
the bed, loosening her hand. It was only a momentary
loss, for she found other wonderful places to touch. The
back of his neck and the breadth of his shoulders. The
long, sleek contours of his back led her fingertips to
beautiful, hard buttocks.

Jeans and boots were peeled and pulled away, but not
panties. Not yet. The barrier they posed was wonderfully frustrating when he touched her there and when he
pressed his hard flesh there and when he rocked and
rocked and rocked his hips against hers.

And, oh, she went soft. As soft as clay. He was hard,
and he would leave the imprint of his body in the
softness of hers, melting her every bone. She was liquid,
hot and seeping into his flesh. He collected her, gathered
her up, up to the quivering brim, and when her essence
spilled, he refilled her, until both of them were at once
spent and replete.

His pain came stealing in during the middle of the
night. The usual dull ache insinuated itself into his brain,
but by the time he came fully awake, he was blind with
it. It hadn't been this bad for a while, and he'd almost
let himself believe it wouldn't be again. He lay still, for
movement hurt, and he made himself remember that it
would pass. Without her knowing, he hoped. Without
her seeing him like this.

But her voice came floating.

"What's wrong?" She touched him. Her hands were
cool. "Trey, you're soaking wet."

"Hot," he mumbled. "Air's not moving."

"You're hurting."

"Just a headache. Shh. It won't last."

"Just?"

He felt her hands on his face, in his hair, and he thought, Don't get scared, Frankie. The monster goes away.

"What can I do?" she said softly. "I have aspirin. Do you have anything stronger?"

"Not with me." She moved away, and he heard the click. "Don't turn the light on!" He shielded his face with his arm and turned from the thing that stabbed more deeply than movement. "Please."

It was dark again, and she was back, whispering, "I'm sorry. I'll get you some aspirin."

He wanted her voice more than the aspirin, but soon he had both. She bathed his face. She held his head in the cool valley between her breasts and stroked him, massaged his temples where the pain was the worst, tended him until it faded.

"How long did it last?" he asked when all that was left was a dull throb.

"Maybe twenty minutes. Does it happen often?"

"It's gotten a lot better. I used to have blackouts. I haven't had one that bad for a while."

"What do you usually take for this?" she asked, and when he started to get up, she said, "Lie still now."

"I try to stick to aspirin. I've got a prescription for codeine, but I…"

He had to tell her. She'd seen the weakness that laid him so low. He would confess to the one that shamed him. "One of the reasons I had to take early retirement was that I got strung out on painkillers."

"So you…"

"Went through drug treatment. The people around me gave me permission to be dependent, you know? They said, 'Who can blame you? You've got a good reason for using.'" His throat went dry, but he continued. She hadn't pulled away from him yet, he thought. "After a while, I didn't need a reason. Preventive medicine, I called it. It was preventing me from making the adjustments, the changes I needed to make in my life."

"Like moving back here?"

"I had to swallow some pride to do that. Connie remarried. I wasn't very good at playing weekend Daddy. She said I could have Tricia with me in the summers once I got myself straightened out, so I decided to try to do that here. My roots are here. I figured I had a family, of sorts." He touched her cheek. "I envy you your family. I always have."

"You were like part of it when we were growing up."

"I should have tried to include Race more. I should have been more…"

She touched her finger to his lips. "You can make all kinds of changes and adjustments, but you can't change what's already happened."

She sensed his thirst. In the dark she found the glass she'd set aside on the bed table and offered him a drink. Gratefully he slaked his thirst. The bout had left him shaking, and he dropped his head back to the pillow, hoping it wasn't too noticeable.

"Are you okay now, with the drugs?" She set the glass away and recovered the cloth she'd used moments ago, dipping it again in the small bowl of water.

"I'm okay without them. But when the pain comes, I still think, isn't this what they're for? Why suffer? I get myself past that thinking, and then I'm okay." She began swabbing his chest with the cool cloth, and he smiled. "You got me past it this time."

"Am I a good distraction?"

"The best." He lifted his hand to touch her cheek, and she turned her lips to the center of his palm and kissed him. "Oh, God, Frankie, you're the best."

Chapter 11

This time, Chuck Two Hawk came looking for Trey.

It was late in the day, and Trey was just finishing up in the barn when Zeppelin's bark announced the approach of a visitor. Trey pushed a wheelbarrow of manure out the side door and saw the police car kicking up a dusty wake as it headed toward the house. Two Hawk must have seen him, too, because he took a sharp turn, skirting the house in favor of the barn. A flock of barn swallows burst into the air, wings churning them out of the way of the roaring engine and yapping dog. Trey tipped the barrow on its front wheel and added the rank load to a rotting pile of the same.

"I've got some news for you," Two Hawk shouted as he alighted from the car. Zeppelin bared his formidable canines and growled. Two Hawk stayed behind the car door. "Ssst. Get away, dog."

"Zep!" Trey whistled, and the dog came running. "He's okay, if the news is good."

"It's information," Two Hawk said. He waited to be sure the dog was no longer interested in him before he approached Trey at the corral gate. He was wearing his blue uniform. This was business. "The kind you asked me for."

Trey was assessing the damage on his final maintenance job for the day. "Could you give me a hand with this gate? I just need to fix this hinge. Then I'm done."

No instructions were needed. Two Hawk held the heavy gate in place while Trey replaced the top hinge bolts. "What have you got for me?" he asked as he lined up the first bolt.

"My brother-in-law, Jimmy Sentinel Horse, over at Crow Agency, he knows your friend Messner." Two Hawk sighted along the top of the gate, leveling it as he spoke. "Jimmy had a deal going where him and another guy had spotted some government surplus equipment they figured on picking up pretty cheap. They were going to bid on a sanitation contract—some wells and septic systems going in on country sites. They got a small loan. All of a sudden, no equipment."

"They sold it out from under them?"

"It didn't show up at the auction. One day they're told it's going to be auctioned. The next day it's, 'What equipment? All we got this month is surplus sewing machines.'"

Two Hawk flexed his knees and shifted the weight of the gate to his shoulder. "Jimmy started looking for another deal on used equipment, but then somebody ran his partner's wife off the road. She hit an approach and got hurt pretty bad. Jimmy got a couple of threatening phone calls. And these guys got a hell of a nerve.

They called him at the police station, where he works. Then somebody shot his dog and left him a note about getting in somebody else's yard. So Jimmy and his friend pulled out, and Messner got the contract."

Trey gave the bolt a few good whacks while he digested all this. Then he propped his forearm against the gate post, wiped the sweat off his nose with his sleeve and looked at Two Hawk. "Is Messner still doing business with Crow Agency?"

"Seems they had a shakeup out there. Transferred some B.I.A. personnel around. Messner pulled up stakes and headed east."

"Somebody wouldn't play ball with him."

"That's what I figure. It would be interesting to know who it was and how he was approached."

Trey drove the hinge bolt home and tossed his mallet into the toolbox on the ground. "Messner's got two Walworth County deputies in his pocket. 'Course, deputy sheriff isn't much of a job around here, so they work construction. Or at least they're on the payroll. One at L & M, and one at Messner Sand and Gravel." Two Hawk glanced up as Trey gave the grate a test push. "Vernon Stoller and Tommy Jenkins," Trey supplied. "You know them?"

"Couple of gun-happy rednecks."

"Sounds like a good description." Trey laid his hand on the top of the gate and eyed Two Hawk. "Level with me, Chuck. Is that what people call me?"

"Nah." Two Hawk's hooded eyes were inscrutable as he scanned the yard for Trey's vehicle. "You got no gun rack in your pickup." There was a hint of smile as he glanced back at Trey.

Trey wondered whether that eliminated the "redneck"

designation along with the "gun-happy" part, but he decided not to push his luck.

"Anyway, along with Stoller and Jenkins, he's got this guy named Sheldon Tate from Montana," Trey reported as he pulled the gate shut and latched it. "I'd be willing to bet that one of those guys was George's visitor the other night, but it must have taken more than one of them to work him over."

He turned, hooked his hands at his hips and squinted into the sinking sun. Here was the bad part, the part that was driving him nuts. "Frankie's been harassed on the highway twice. Once by the two deputies."

Two Hawk wasn't surprised. "That's kind of a pastime in some of these off-reservation towns, Latimer. Didn't you know that?"

"I've, uh…gained a new perspective just lately."

"She's damn good-looking, too."

"And she's gonna take these guys to the cleaners for what they did, whether they had anything to do with the assault or not."

Two Hawk gave no response. Trey felt like saying, *So what if she's good looking?* But he decided Two Hawk hadn't meant anything by it.

"Did Jimmy tell you anything else?" he asked. "Like, has any of Messner's competition ever wound up dead?"

"No. Just scared into backing out." Two Hark nodded as he folded his arms over his chest. "They go after a guy's dog, though, that's getting serious."

What? "Didn't they go after the one guy's wife?"

"Well, that was just a warning."

Trey stared. Two Hawk finally smiled.

"You've got a weird sense of humor, Two Hawk."

"That's part of the new perspective, my friend." He

laid a beefy hand on Trey's shoulder, a move that took
Trey by surprise. It also made him feel as though he
were being accepted. Maybe he'd passed a test.

Two Hawk stepped over to his side, folded his arms
again and scanned the shadowed hills as he elaborated,
on the level this time. "What goes on isn't funny. We've
been putting up with it for one hell of a long time, and
there's a lot of white guys thinking we don't know any
better. That's what we think is funny."

"If you'd seen Frankie after—" Trey's eyes rested on
the big square butte as his mind, never far from her
now, drifted back.

"I saw George after they first brought him into the
hospital," Two Hawk said. "And, I gotta admit, I thought
it was Race. Frankie thought it was Race, but she still
wanted you on the case." He made a clucking sound.
"Yep." He sighed dramatically and eyed Trey askance.
"Must be those pretty blue eyes of yours."

"Gimme a break, Two Hawk."

"Okay, you turned out to be more than just a pretty
face." He grinned, eyes alight. "That was your break,
Latimer. Treasure it."

Trey shook his head and laughed.

"See there?" Two Hawk thumped him on the chest
with the back of his hand. "You're learning. Don't take
yourself so damn seriously."

"I wasn't going to be too serious about this job when
I took it, to be honest with you."

"That new perspective looks good on you."
Abruptly, he turned back to the matter at hand. "I've
tried to get them to keep a man at the clinic as much
as I could, but we're shorthanded. If we could get
some kind of hard evidence linking Messner or the

federal contracts to the assault, we could interest the FBI pretty quick."

"They're going to try to silence George, sooner or later."

"They'll have to."

"We've got one thing going for us," Trey said. "They've left a trail a mile wide. They're continuing to operate the way they have before. Obviously *they* don't take us too damn seriously."

"You and me?" Two Hawk chortled. "'A temporary sheriff and a B.I.A. cop,' they'll be saying. 'What are they going to do to stop us?'"

"Frankie has the right idea. Flush them out." Trey snatched his tool box off the ground, then added, "But damn, I don't want her in on it."

"She's already in on it. You know that." Two Hawk's hand landed on Trey's shoulder again, and he cocked his hip and took a picture-this stance. "I think it's time to use the old warrior tactic. Couple of braves appear on the hill. Dumb bluecoats chase after them." His free hand became a horse, headed toward Rattlesnake Butte. "They get over the hill, and the war party's waiting for them, just grinning to beat hell."

"So we're the war party," Trey concluded. Two Hawk nodded. "And Frankie's the brave."

"Frankie and George."

"A woman and a guy who's laid up in the hospital?"

The description didn't require any affirmation, so Two Hawk gave none.

Trey walked over to his truck and dropped the metal toolbox into the back. He braced his arms on the side of the pickup box and considered the options. There were damn few. "Have you heard of any warriors who actually used this old Indian trick?"

"Saw it with my own eyes. It worked great." Two Hawk waited for Trey's over-the-shoulder look before he added, "Crazy Horse, played by Anthony Quinn."

"Let's go see what my partner has to say." Trey pushed himself away from the pickup and pulled off his leather work gloves. "Her sense of humor is a lot like yours."

Trey's partner wasn't where she was supposed to be. One of two places, she'd said, the school or her house. She wasn't going out on the highway alone. Dusk was drawing down as her younger sister, Crystal, answered the door.

"Frankie's been trying to call you," she told Trey through the screen door. "I think she wanted you to go up to Fort Yates with her. She's already left."

"I've been working in the barn all afternoon. Can't hear the phone out there. When did she leave?"

"Little while ago."

"How long?" Two Hawk put in. "Minutes? Hours?"

"Maybe twenty or thirty minutes."

Checking his watch was an automatic response for Trey. "She's still on the road. Why didn't she wait for me? I told her I'd be here before dark."

"She said to give you this." Crystal pushed the door open and handed him a note, which wasn't going to be easy to read in the waning light. But Crystal was making no offers to let the two men in. "She seemed kinda nervous, and she wouldn't take me with her. I'm supposed to go back over to my auntie's house and not hang around here. Weird, huh?"

"Pretty weird."

"She's gettin' that way lately," Crystal commented as she closed the inside door and tested the lock. She looked up at Trey, as though considering his merits. He remembered twelve-year-old Frankie, same long braids, same big chocolate eyes. Same mischievous grin. "I think she's lovesick, myself," Crystal said.

As they walked back to the patrol car, the two men watched the girl run across the graveled driveway and gain admittance into another small white house. Trey slid into the passenger seat, tore into the envelope and tilted the note toward the dome light.

Why don't you answer your phone, Latimer? I'm getting strange calls on mine. First one didn't say anything, just played the nursery rhyme "Georgie Porgie." Second one just breathed and hung up. Meet me at the hospital.

"When I get my hands on this woman—"

"Yeah?"

Trey handed Two Hawk the note and grumbled while the policeman scanned it. "Sure as hell, somebody's out there waiting for her. If that damn rubber-band-powered car of hers breaks down—"

Two Hawk handed the note back and turned the key in the ignition. "Which road would she take?"

"She was in a hurry. She'd take the shortcut with all the potholes and not a soul on the road but her and that—"

"I'll send a car the other way," Two Hawk promised, reaching for the handset on the two-way radio. "I know what you're thinking, man. We won't be far behind her."

Two Hawk made good time, considering they didn't want to miss anything along the way and they'd lost the daylight. Trey watched for her car, fully expecting their headlights to suddenly illuminate it in the ditch beside the road. He prayed they wouldn't, and he prayed that if they did, it would be sitting on all four tires, and she would be sitting inside, safe. That awful dream of hers was in his head. Wherever she was, she needed to stay put. Something didn't want her there.

The hospital was quiet. People were heading out for Labor Day weekend if they could, and much of the town was deserted. Only the seriously ill and the stuck-on-duty would be around. Frankie said hello to Janet Silk as she passed her in the hall. "What's George up to?" she asked.

"I'll let you see for yourself," Janet said as she headed down the hall. "I've got a call light on."

The door to George's room was closed, and Frankie heard what seemed to be the only voices in the building. She expected to find George watching TV.

What she did not expect to find was Short Creep, the deputy from Walworth County. He was without his mirrored sunglasses and his tall buddy, but he did have his pistol. It was holstered, but a clear and present danger, nevertheless. The two men were definitely not watching the movie on TV. Frankie's stomach twisted itself into a knot.

"What are you doing here?" she asked quietly.

"Come in and shut the door, Frances." George was sitting up in bed, and he didn't seem to be alarmed.

"You're not authorized to…" Frankie stepped closer to the bed. "I mean, George's visitors are limited to…just certain people."

"It's all right, Frankie," George said. "I guess Vernon and I worked together on a project for Craig Pratt once. But I can't remember. Jeez, I just—" he lifted his shoulders and sighed in a helpless gesture "—can't remember any damn thing these days."

Stoller got up and closed the door. Frankie moved to the bedside. "These people you once worked with seem to be coming out of the woodwork all of a sudden, don't they, George?" she said.

Stoller walked back to his chair and sat down, resting his elbows on his knees. He gave George a gap-toothed smile. "Everybody likes George. I was pretty upset when I heard what happened to him, and I got to thinking maybe this bunch of punks we picked up last week for trying to roll some poor old drunk might have been the same ones who did this to George." He passed the gun back and forth between his hands, as if he were playing with a toy as he spoke. "So I was just asking him if he thought he could remember, maybe, if he saw a face."

Frankie concentrated on keeping her voice steady. "I don't have any trouble remembering faces— Vernon, is it?" *Never let a dog smell fear.* "And I don't know what your game is now, but George is in no condition to—"

The deputy cradled the pistol in both hands and slowly moved them up and down, as though testing the gun's weight. "One of the things they tell you when they give you a badge is that you can't carry a concealed weapon. So I don't. I keep it where people can see it. Then they don't usually give me much trouble." He looked up at Frankie. "I'm not playing games, Frances. I just want to see if George can somehow reach back and remember something about whoever beat him up. Like maybe they were kids or something. And, you know, just *tell* us that, so we can get on with the job and lay this thing to rest."

"Right now all I'm worried about is getting back—" George made a production of bracing his hands on either side of his hips to push himself up straighter. "Damn, I hit my call button by accident. Frankie, flip that switch up there so it'll turn off."

He looked up at her. It was an unexpected, direct and meaningful eye contact with more of George's mind than she had realized was there. He shifted his good eye quickly to the lever above him, then back to her. She complied.

He squirmed around as if he'd lost control again, fumbling near the call button. "Oh, I did it again. So damn clumsy on my left side. Hit it again, would you, Frankie?"

"We don't want anybody else in here, George." It was Stoller's turn to cast Frankie a pointed look. "We got enough people already."

"Maybe you should go, Vernon," she said.

"Maybe you guys should leave that button alone so we don't get these nurses running in here when we don't need them."

Still carrying his pistol at his side, Vernon went to the door.

Trey pushed his way through a fire door and greeted Janet Silk, who was on her way from the OB wing back to the nurses' station.

"Is Frankie here?"

Janet jerked her chin toward the familiar door down the hall. "She's in George's room."

A male orderly, standing next to the desk, offered an additional piece of news. "Your deputy's in there, too."

Trey glanced at Two Hawk, then back to the orderly. "My *deputy?*"

"*I* didn't see anyone else go in there," Janet countered.

The orderly shrugged. "He came in a few minutes ago, showed me his badge and said the sheriff had sent him."

Trey managed a quarter turn away from the desk

before Two Hawk grabbed his arm. At the same time he asked the orderly, "What kind of badge?"

The young man shrugged. "A police kind of badge. You know, I just glanced. No uniform, but he had a holster on his hip. First he went in, then Frankie a few minutes later."

"What happened to the man we had posted?" Two Hawk asked.

"He left about five, I guess."

"The door's been closed? No one left? No sounds?" Trey figured no one had been watching, even though Janet and the orderly dutifully nodded, then shook their heads.

Janet glanced at the call board. "George's call light is on. Wait, now it's off."

"On again," the orderly chimed in. "Somebody has to be turning it on and then flicking the wall switch."

"Call the station," Two Hawk told Janet. "Tell them to send us some backup. You," he told the orderly quietly. "Anybody in these rooms close by?" The young man pointed to a room down the hall. "Go down there and see that he stays put," Two Hawk directed.

The orderly trotted stiffly down the hall on crepe tiptoes.

Trey and Two Hawk exchanged signals, and Two Hawk stationed himself flat against the wall next to George's door. He drew his service revolver and pointed the barrel toward the ceiling. Trey's gun was in his holster. He could hear the television, but he wished he could see through the door. He imagined George, Frankie and a man with a gun. But who was where?

"Police," he announced as he opened the door. "Everybody re—" He was looking down the barrel of a .57 Magnum, but he completed his statement as he accounted for Frankie and George on the other side of the room. "Everybody relax. Why don't you put that down, deputy? Let's talk."

Use your head. Don't lose it. String this guy along and forget about the damn gun.

"I don't think so. I haven't done nothing." Wild-eyed, the deputy took a step toward the door. "I wasn't the one that frisked the lady. I just want to get out of here, so you just step back, Latimer, and let me—"

Trey stepped back slowly, both hands chest level, palms out. He set his jaw and and stared Stoller down. His temple began its throbbing as the gunman followed him, step for step.

This was the short guy. The one who was all talk. The one Race said he doubted had ever fired a gun.

Another step back.

Come on, dummy. Bring me the gun. Bring it along, now. Keep it coming.

Stoller stepped across the threshold. Two Hawk placed the barrel of his revolver next to Stoller's temple and advanced a bullet into the chamber. "Put the gun down or you're dead."

Stoller's eyes shifted, but he knew better than to move his head. Sweat beaded on his brow. His nostrils flared. Trey pushed Stoller's gun barrel down and away, and the man's hand went slack. Trey disarmed him.

"I know this guy, Trey," George shouted. "I remember him real good."

"From where, George?"

"From Mobridge that night. I remember thinking how you could drive a truck between his front teeth." George threw back the covers and started out of bed. "I didn't want nobody getting hurt, so I just played along, hoping somebody would notice something was wrong."

Trey's heart thudded in his ears as his eyes sought Frankie's through the doorway. "I figured that was my partner signaling with the call light."

The gladness in her eyes sang back to him. "That was George's idea."

"I wasn't the one," Stoller wailed. "I didn't hit him. Not once."

"You offered me a drink," George continued excitedly as he swung his legs over the side of the bed. "I was walking down the street toward my pickup, and you stopped me. You handed me a pint, and I told you no, remember? No thanks, I said. Finally I took a pull on it just to be sociable, and I don't know what, but something sure packed a wallop."

Janet Silk peeked around the door of the office behind the nurses' station. "I've called the police station," she said, and then she tucked her head back in like a turtle.

Trey pushed Stoller back inside the room and made him face the wall. "Is this one of the jerks who stopped you on the highway, Frankie?" Stoller started to turn his head, and Trey slammed him against the wall. "You know the position, deputy."

Trey glanced over his shoulder as he searched Stoller for more weapons. "Is this the one, Frankie?"

"He's one of them. He was the bystander."

"The bystander, huh?" Two Hawk handed him the cuffs, and Trey jerked Stoller's arms into place behind his back. "This lady's my partner, deputy. Did you enjoy watching your partner humiliate mine?"

"N-no. Like the lady says, I didn't do nothin'."

"You didn't do *nothin'*, huh?" Trey turned to Two Hawk. "What kind of rights we got for somebody who *didn't do nothin'?*"

Two Hawk could hardly get the Miranda warning in edgewise while Stoller ran at the mouth. "It was Jenkins and Tate who beat George up," he claimed. "I'm not taking the rap for any of this."

"You work for Messner?" Trey asked. Stoller nodded. "What about my father? You work for my father at all?"

"Messner hired me. Tate gave all the orders. Tate told us he'd seen George in the hospital, and that George didn't remember anything, probably never would. And anyway, I wasn't the one who hit him. I thought we were just going to get him drunk and scare him a little, but Tate, he dragged him back in the alley and got started beating on him. Wouldn't quit."

Stoller glanced at George and Frankie, for whom the story was clearly spellbinding. He turned back to Trey. "I wasn't gonna shoot nobody. I called, see, I thought she was home. I was supposed to scare her, scare him. Get them to back off those bids. That's what we were getting paid for, I thought. Just putting a scare into them."

"What were you going to do if George recognized you right off?"

"Tate said it wouldn't matter, as long as we backed each other up." Stoller tried to step closer to Trey, but Two Hawk jerked back on him and held him fast. "See, I didn't do nothing, so if you guys get Tate, I'll testify. But you better get him right away, 'cause otherwise I might be dead."

Feeling elated with his catch, Trey shook his aching head. "I have never seen a bird more willing to sing without an attorney present than you are, deputy."

"I didn't do nothing, that's why." Two Hawk was moving Stoller along, and the man was still talking.

"I'm the only one he saw, and I didn't do nothing. See, that's what bothered me."

Two Indian policemen appeared in the hallway.

"We got a place to put this guy?" Two Hawk asked them as he motioned for them to lend a hand. "He's the kind that likes to push Indians around."

As Stoller was taken away, Frankie moved to Trey's side. He put his arm around her shoulders. "Hey, Two Hawk," he said as the policeman started out the door. "I don't mind being part of the war party, but the next time we use a different brave."

"I'm all for that." Two Hawk grinned. "We'll have to call her Steals Thunder Woman."

"I'll be over in a few minutes," Trey promised. Two Hawk nodded and followed his fellow officers.

"Brave?" Frankie questioned.

"Yeah." Trey turned to take her in his arms. "Except you forgot to make sure the war party was ready."

"What war party?" Frankie slid her arms around him and squeezed. "Where were you, Latimer? I kept calling and calling…"

"Where was *I*? Where were *you*? I told you I'd pick you up at—" She was a beautiful, beautiful, sight to see. All he wanted to do was hold her close and keep her safe.

He shook his head and sighed. "I had my eyes glued to the ditches on the way up here, Frankie. I was scared they'd try to run you off the road again. You had no business—" He looked up and saw George standing—a little hip-shot, granted, and supporting himself on the tray table—but *standing* next to the bed and grinning at him.

"What am I going to do with her, George?"

"I'm waiting to see if you're gonna kiss her."

Trey looked down at the woman in his arms, smiled, and gratefully obliged.

Chapter 12

Working weekends was one of the things Trey had been trying to get away from. That and guns. He hadn't succeeded much lately. Just take the job temporarily, the county commissioner had said. You've been a big city cop, so this'll be a piece of cake. Hardly anything to do, what with the B.I.A. police and the State Highway Patrol and all those guys. Once in a while somebody's cows get out on the road, or somebody might have a trespasser, but usually it's a pretty dull job.

Well, he'd worked damn near the whole Labor Day weekend, almost around the clock. On the basis of Stoller's statement Trey had arrested Jenkins and put out a warrant for Tate. Two Hawk had brought in the local FBI agents, who were anxious to be able to pin something on Dermot Messner. Trey figured the Aberdeen Area Office was in for the same kind of shakeup they'd had at Crow Agency. A good, thorough, government housecleaning. The kind that made room for a new band of bureaucrats to move in. Some would be corruptible, some wouldn't. But there would always be guys like Messner around trying to figure out who was who.

According to Two Hawk, that was why Trey might want to think about running for sheriff in November. In the last three days he'd only brought the subject up about half a dozen times. Trey figured he must have passed another of Two Hawk's tests that night at the hospital. Hospital tests were not his favorite kind, but at least this time no one had drawn any blood.

As he pulled through the gates of United Tribes Training Center, he decided he would think about maybe running, just for one term. He'd tested the waters, and he hadn't gotten his head blown apart. He hadn't frozen when he'd faced a gun. He hadn't blacked out. Things were looking up.

But he hadn't seen much of Frankie in the past several days, and he was about to come apart on that score. He'd called her as often as he could get near a phone, and the sound of her voice made him ache bad, and not in his head. When he'd run out of excuses, he'd finally told her that.

"I'm just calling because I like hearing you breathe close to my ear. Could you do it for me…Frankie?"

"I *am*."

"Do it again, a little harder," he said, grinning up at a fluorescent ceiling light in the B.I.A. Police Station.

"I'm sitting here at my parent's house, Latimer. I've got kids…here, listen to this." He heard one kid yelp, another one laugh, and somebody whining to use the phone. "Hear that? They're all over me, so you'll have to request a different tune for now." She paused, then added quietly, "I'll play your favorite one for you some other time."

"I love you, Frankie."

"You…you what?"

"I said I love you. I don't care who hears me."

"Oh." She sounded stunned. "Are you sure?"

"Absolutely. You're not surprised, are you?"

"Well…" Then the small distant voice became Frankie's again. "You picked a fine time to tell me. How can I tell if you mean it if I can't see your eyes?"

"This is not one of those white lies, Frankie." There was a long pause. No yelps, no giggles, no whines. "So what about it?"

Her unsteady sigh made his mouth go dry. "I love you, too, Trey. I always have."

Wolf calls, war whoops and a chirpy "Frankie loves Tre-ey" came zinging over the phone line.

"Now see what you've done to me," she said, laughing.

"You oughta see what you've done to me."

She'd made him happy. She'd made him smile at a lightbulb and draw hearts around two little stick figures on his police report, in triplicate. She had said they were bringing George up for the last night of the powwow, and it was going to be a big night for her. She would be wearing her grandmother's dress.

United Tribes was an old army post that had been turned into an Indian training center. The big brick buildings that had once been barracks now housed classrooms, and the old parade ground was the scene of what was probably one of the biggest Indian encampments since the Little Big Horn. And they were camped there with the same peaceful purpose in mind. Socializing and celebrating. Labor Day was the end of the powwow season.

Trey vowed to make this the beginning of a lifetime of seasons for Frankie and him. He wanted to be watching her dance when she was one of the old women in the circle and he was one of the old men on the sidelines. Their daughter would wear the beautiful beaded dress, and their granddaughter, dressed in a fringed shawl and satin ribbons, would be looking forward to her turn.

He parked his pickup and made his way toward the bowery, which was a much larger and more permanent structure than the one at Bullhead. But it was still a circle. And the sound of the singers pounding on the drum still seeped into his blood.

He found Lannie and George first. George was in a wheelchair, which he said he really didn't need. "Just wanna see what kind of muscle your sister's got," he teased. "I'll be on my feet by Christmas."

"If you do your exercises," Lannie reminded him.

"She said she won't marry me unless I can walk her back down the aisle and kick up my heels at the wedding dance," George told Trey.

"I did not." Lannie shook her head, laughing, and Trey realized how pretty she was when she laughed.

"So you should see me," George said. "I get on that little walker they got me using, and I *really* race her around that apartment of hers."

"Speaking of Race," Lannie said, "he called me. Said to tell you he read about you in the paper." Their eyes exchanged a quiet sadness.

"He's okay, then?"

"I think so. Have you seen Dad?"

Trey shook his head.

"After this is all over, maybe you and he can…"

"Maybe so," Trey said. "There's a lot of legal stuff yet to come down the pike, but I don't think he's guilty of anything but looking the other way, which they don't usually put anybody in jail for."

The conversation was cut short by the announcement of the women's traditional dance. Trey knew where he could find Frankie. He pushed George's wheelchair past the bleachers, but he sought his own vantage point from which to watch her perform. He didn't want to be distracted by anything or anyone, and he didn't want her to see him until her dance was over.

The music and the solemnity of the circle transported him as they had before. Frankie's loveliness filled his heart. Something old, something new, he thought. The timeless old dress and the proud young woman who made the best of things. He could do that, too. It had taken him a long time to come to her, but he had come full circle.

When the dance was over, he stepped out of the shadows. Her face brightened when she saw him. She lifted her skirt and quickened her step.

"You were wonderful," he told her as she stepped close to him and discreetly took his hand.

"I like your new hat."

He touched the silver-belly-colored brim. "You don't think it makes me look kind of redneckish, do you?"

"Redneckish?" Her laughter bubbled. "You've gotta make up your mind, Latimer. You can be a redneck, or you can be squaw man. But you can't be both."

"I brought my own tent," he said.

"Well, let's walk, then."

They strolled amid the crowd, hands clasped between

them. She slid him a sideways glance. "Are you hungry? Want some frybread?"

"Not really." He did a little rubbernecking, surveying the grounds. This powwow looked more like a county fair, with a complete outer circle of souvenir booths and Indian taco stands. "Where's the Ferris wheel?"

"There isn't one. We're uptown here. There's a shopping mall." He laughed, and she asked, "Do you know how to pitch a tent?"

"I've never camped much. I just bought the thing."

"It's a good thing you have an experienced partner."

He squeezed her hand and grinned. He figured they probably looked like a couple of starry-eyed high-school kids, holding hands and smiling at each other like this. But he was glad they weren't.

"What's a squaw man?" he asked. "Or do I want to know that?"

"It's not a threat to your masculinity."

"That's a relief." Then, as casually as he could manage, "Does it have anything to do with us getting married?"

She stopped them both in their tracks and looked up at him. His eyes met hers, and he stood his ground, trying to prepare for anything. With Frankie, he just never knew.

"On one condition."

He hadn't exactly asked, and already there was a condition. "What's that?"

"If you're going to ask me, I want flowers first."

"Flowers?" The corners of his mouth twitched.

"And then, if you want sons in return, well, okay."

Laughing, he picked her up and spun around with her like a crazy man, for all the world to see.

Laughing, too, she threw her arms around him and

kissed him, for all the world to see. And then she whispered in his ear, "They've got flowers in the refrigerator at the grocery store."

"E'en it?" he teased, letting her slide down the front of him as she laughed over his use of the local "is that so?" idiom. "Let's go find some."

* * * * *

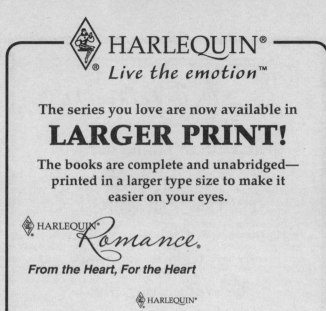

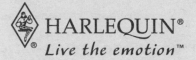

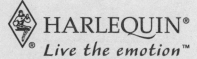

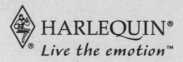